THE WRATH OF NIGHT

VIOLA TEMPEST

CONTENTS

THE WRATH OF NIGHT

VIOLA TEMPEST

CHAPTER
ONE

"No! Father!" Finley shouted in dismay, but her mother wrestled her in place.

"You're not getting on this ship, Sharpe!" the man holding the boy called out. "I've had your access revoked."

"You know I won't let you do this, not to them and not to my family!" Finley's father shouted, and she'd never heard him so angry. "The people deserve better; they're humans, not animals!"

"You never had the right vision for this project,

Sharpe. Your services have been appreciated, but we'll take it from here."

"If you think—"

A gunshot rang out, so close that Finley's ears started to ring, and everything went dim for a moment. She didn't hear her mother scream, but she did see her collapse onto the ground. Her father lied supine on the floor, motionless, with dark red blood pooling around his head.

She stared into his lifeless eyes for only a second, before choking on a scream that ripped its way free from her throat.

Finley ran for him, to grab onto him, to hug him, something. Anything to stop what had just happened. She was young, but not too young to understand what death was. How irreversible it was. But then someone pulled at her arms. It wasn't her mother; she was weeping with her head on father's still chest.

Finley flailed wildly until a familiar voice faded into her awareness.

"Come on, Finley! We have to go!"

It's the boy. She looked at him, bewildered.

He'd never broken a pinkie swear before. Not once. But he said everything was going to be okay. But it wasn't. It couldn't be. Because her father was dead. And the man who had shot him… The man who had shot him was leading him away.

She thrashed and threw his arm off of body. "No!" Finley screamed. "Get away from me! Let me go!"

He looked shocked, but for once, she didn't care. All she cared about was getting to her mother and father, so everything could be okay again. She thought the boy was going to say something else, but before he could, the older man, gun still in hand, began dragging him back. He said nothing, just stared at her as he went. When he finally disappeared into one of the giant metal ships, she ran over to her parents.

Her father's skin was cold when she touched him, and his red blood leaked onto her fingers like the darkest shade of crimson. Her mother was also now still, no longer crying, but also not moving.

"Mother?" Finley asked quietly, and the woman jumped, sniffling as if she had forgotten her daughter was still there.

Her tears fell heavily as she looked at Finley with watery blank eyes. She was too young to understand what it meant, but her instincts told her it was bad, whispers of voids that couldn't be climbed out of.

Their quiet moment of horror was disturbed when the gunshots, which had faded into the background, became more pronounced, and the voices of the crowd seemed to swell. The metal fence gave a loud groan before snapping, the metal wires pinging away. The people rushed forward like a river bursting through its dam, and the sound of thousands of feet became the drums of the rain.

Her mother didn't move until the people were upon them, rushing past, some avoiding their hunched forms, and others trampling right through. Finley was scared that she was about to drown amongst them when her mother finally snapped out of it. She grabbed the girl, rougher than she ever had, and hoisted her toward her chest.

"Come on, sweetie. Let's get you out of here," she

murmured, but for some reason, it didn't comfort her daughter. Instead, Finley had a sick feeling that it was the last time she would be in her mother's arms.

There were screams everywhere as the people wrestled with armed guards to get onto the ships. Three of the five had already been breached, the people scattering into space like cockroaches disappearing through a hole in the wall. It seemed like the chaos would go on forever when the loudest siren she had ever heard blasted its way across the tarmac, her eardrums screaming in protest.

Everything seemed to stop, the people froze, and silence fell upon them like a terrible blanket.

"Count down initiated," a clean female voice chanted. The stillness remained. "One minute until launch," she spoke again, her voice echoing.

It was only then that Finley realized she hadn't even begun to see the extent of human terror... until that moment. The screaming started up again, and this time, it didn't seem to lull or dip. People fought ruthlessly to scramble onto the ships, whose doors were now slowly and undeniably shutting.

Finley jumped when her mother screamed, "No! You will not die today!"

Her mother then started pushing through the crowd while pulling Finley behind her, using her bag as the battering ram of a knight. Except, this wasn't fun, and it wasn't a fantasy movie. She could feel people's hands grabbing at her, their fingernails scraping along her scalp and back. But despite her cries of pain, her mother didn't stop; she didn't give in.

The doors were nearly closed now. Only enough space for three people… two people… one person…

Her mother was slim. She might have been able to squeeze through still, and they were nearly there. So close. They could almost touch it.

Suddenly, her mother fell, and Finley flew from her grasp, hitting the concrete with a thud, and the air was knocked from her chest. Finley lied there gasping, staring up at the towering metal beast above her like some sentient god. She could have lied there forever, fallen asleep right amid the mob, staring up at the thing that was so incomprehensible to her young mind. But then, her mother was there again, pulling her up.

"No, mother." Finley groaned but followed suit.

However, the gap between the doors were too small for them both now. They had missed their chance to run toward safety. Finley couldn't comprehend what her mother had planned until she found herself being lifted into the air.

She squirmed and yelled, grabbing for her mother. "Please!" she begged. "No, don't make me go. Not alone!"

The child screamed and cried, but nothing seemed to work. Once her mother had perched her daughter's small frame inside the slowly closing door, she shoved in a bag. For one terrifying moment, Finley couldn't see her mother, and she scrambled to move the damn bag so she could climb back out again, back into her mother's comforting arms.

But by the time she managed to move the bag's heavy weight, the gap was too small for her to fit through. She wailed, pushing her arm through the gap.

"Mother!" She wept, grabbing for the last remaining parent she had left.

But her mother just smiled up at her, tears running down her cheeks. She thought she saw her mother mouth something to her, but it was too loud to hear with all the sounds of a strange rumbling, the people's cries, the gunshots, the alarms. Her mother's mouth kept repeating the same silent words, right up until she was swallowed by the crowd outside.

Finley stared at where her mother had once been, arm outstretched, until the closing door threatened to snap it in half, and with one last sob, she pulled it back in.

The door closed with one quiet, damnable, *whoosh!*

And then… darkness enveloped her.

———

Sixteen years later…

Finley woke up the same way she always woke up, slowly, like swimming through quicksand. She always wished for that sudden jolting wakefulness, the type that people got when they were startled awake by a nightmare, but she was never that lucky.

No, she had to drag herself out from her nightmares, pulling her limbs achingly slowly from their sticky clutches. It was why she never slept in complete darkness, always with her curtains open to let in the dim light of the city beyond.

It's not that she was afraid of the dark; there were few things she feared these days, but the claustrophobia it invited in was suffocating. And when the nightmares that she was fleeing from were actually her memories? Well, let's just say it made them that much harder to banish.

She climbed out of bed slowly, her head still foggy, a headache already pounding behind her eyes. It was always the same when she dreamt of home, always the same scenes and screams following her from the past and into the now.

It was annoying, and it always ruined her mornings.

Trying to reinforce her mood with the irritation rather than the despair that still tried to cling onto her after so many years, Finley walked over to the small bathroom attached to her room, flicking on the lights and squinting when the orange bulb tried to kill her with its beams. Eyes watering, she tried her best to brush her teeth blind, succeeding in only dropping the paste into the sink twice.

Her morning could only get better.

But still, she couldn't shake the sound of the old man's voice from her dream, talking to her father. He had called him by his last name, Sharpe, and mentioned working with him, and yet, he ultimately killed him. It had been so long since that the thought failed to sadden her as it used to. Now, it only filled her with a consuming curiosity. She wanted to know why. What her father had done to warrant his death, and how it played into everything else that happened.

She still used her family's last name.

Finley Sharpe. Ha. The name was apt, almost like calling a circle round. The name was more of a descriptor for her than a last name. She supposed that, in another life, perhaps the name would've been just that, the thing that came after her first name. Maybe the source of some embarrassment, perhaps some light childhood bullying in the schoolyard.

Instead, what the name Sharpe meant to her, to the people, was one of great responsibility, of weight. It sat upon her shoulders like some overindulgent beast, consuming all it could see with no thought to the consequence upon her shaking back. It was self-pity, really, the whining of someone who knew they could have less, much less, and so never voiced their woes out loud for the fear of realizing how privileged they really were.

Get it together, Sharpe, she told herself—she had work to do.

Her tired eyes looked back at her in the bathroom mirror, accusatory and blank. It seemed that even her own reflection had no sense of sympathy for her plight. Under the harsh light above her, she looked washed out, her dark brown hair messy, and her tattoos stark against too pale skin.

On good days, she felt powerful, a motorcycle-riding badass that no one could fuck with. But in those small moments, early in the morning when her dreams still seemed to coat her skin with an invisible layer of grime, she felt empty, like so much of it was just a mask she wore to protect herself. And no matter what she did, she still felt as helpless as she had that night, so long ago…

She itched to get on her motorbike and just ride, ride until her hands were numb, and she could feel nothing but the wind on her face, and her blood rushing through her veins as her bike rumbled against the ground beneath her. Ride to absolutely nowhere, just moving for the sake of moving. She adored her bike. It was a metal masterpiece, but she loved it most for the illusion of freedom that it gave her.

Trying to ignore the echoes of those screams still pulling at her from her restless sleep, Finley stepped away from the mirror and turned to her wardrobe, ready to suit up and face the day. She'd always found that the best cure for an overworked mind was to fill her time with distractions until it was so full that she could barely breathe past every stress and strain. It was almost unbearable, but it was still better than what beckoned to her every time she closed her eyes. The screams. The fire.

She shut down those last thoughts with finality as she slipped on her leather pants, along with a plain top, and tied her hair up into a ponytail. She had a lot to do today, rounds to make in the alleys that surrounded her small run-down apartment, and lots of people to check on. That's what the streets were for, a second home for Finley to look after. The people who lived there were her flock, and she protected them as she would her own.

Looking at her alarm clock, she realized it was much later than she had thought, and with a curse, she grabbed her red leather jacket from her breakfast bar stool while simultaneously trying to step into her boots. She nearly fell over twice, and she was sure it took longer than it would have to just put them on one after another. But hey, she wasn't perfect.

With one last longing look at the box of cereal on her kitchen counter, she opened her front door to leave, her head already busy with calculating which citizens she would be checking up on that day.

She lived in an old apartment that sat across the canal. It was in the "Hopeless District," as people liked to call the area filled with the poor and the homeless, but it was one of the nicer establishments there—at least, everything was still intact. It was also a place where no one knew she lived, except for an exceptional few whom she trusted explicitly, and she knew they would die before giving away her location.

As someone who championed the underdogs, she often ran into trouble with the top pooch, and it helped to have somewhere she could retreat to.

If any of her people needed to contact her, they'd wait in a secure location—which she visited every day at the same time.

Which was also why the note folded neatly on her doorstep was so puzzling to Finley.

She never got mail. The small amount of electricity her home had was powered illegally by the canal it sat over, and she'd bought the building outright. It's not like she had any friends who could afford a pen and paper, let alone a postage stamp.

She picked it up and gazed around suspiciously, but there was no movement in the alley except for the constant billow of smog that filled the entirety of the city. When she'd decided that it was unlikely to be some sort of ambush, she opened the note carefully.

Her irritation spiked when she saw what was on it.

Fucking cryo glyphs.

And there was only one person she knew who could read them.

CHAPTER
TWO

Finley took a sharp left at the end of the alley and charged down the main boulevard of the Hopeless District—if she could even call it that. The main street in this part of town was dirty and mostly unused, with empty shops long invaded by the homeless for shelter. The few establishments that were still standing were forced to sell their essentials for dirt cheap, and sometimes not even that.

To any other person, they might be uncomfortable in the area. They'd probably cringe at the garbage that laid strewn across the pavement and flinch when they saw the rats that crawled out from the sewers, some of them as big as small dogs.

And Finley could admit, the place had seen better days. But having grown up knowing nothing else, it felt like home, no matter the squalor. Of course, the people here, including herself, would love for the place to look better—they didn't enjoy the dirt and filth. But they knew better than to dream of clean clothes and fresh meals. In this city, if someone arrived poor, they stayed that way.

She'd heard from some of the older folks in the community that in the old world, which she had few and unpleasant memories of, people could rise above their poverty—though they always complained about it being harder than it should've been. The idea baffled her all the same because there were absolutely no classes in the great Roseallan City. Just those who had it all, and those who had absolutely nothing.

The name was given to the city by its founders—a bunch of rich idiots who had built the ships that took the last remains of humanity from Earth, across space, and to their new, albeit lacking, home on the Planet Garwick. A city they named after the great founder, with hopes of creating a better life for those who deserved it.

Finley also heard that on the old planet, humans had colonized across the entire thing, moving across the seas until there were very little land left that wasn't filled with a human horde. She couldn't even begin to imagine something like that now. Roseallan City was the only city established on Garwick, and it was surrounded by a large wall along the perimeter to keep out the Antiqua—the bloodthirsty virus-infected humans that had become cannibals after losing all their cognitive ability.

She had been told that it was because of the Antiqua that the humans had to flee the old world in the first place. The virus had spread like wildfire across the planet, awakening the long-dead and killing the new, each one rising as a brand new, unrelenting terrifying creature, hungry for human flesh.

A few managed to get on one of the five great ships that brought the remaining humans here, bringing the plague with them to the new planet. It was because of it that Roseallan City was a barricaded city. The months of establishing the city had been hard, and many had died in the fight to protect themselves. Nearly half the people who had come from Earth perished, all turning into Antiqua, and probably still roaming around in the wastelands, waiting for someone desperate or foolish enough to leave.

It was why none of the poor and homeless had ever tried to leave, to start anew somewhere else where money wasn't an object, and people could live in harmony and survive off the land. Instead, they were trapped here, just as the rich were trapped. It just happened that their cage was a lot nicer than the people who lived here in the Hopeless District.

Finley waved to Benny Otawa, the owner of the corner shop at the end of the boulevard, and he smiled a crooked grin. He was a lovely old man in his fifties, who had come to Roseallan City with a decent fortune. But after his wife, Linda, died, he dedicated himself to helping those less fortunate than himself. He could've been living amongst the other rich, enjoying his old age with comfort. But instead, he sold ready-to-eat meals and blankets for cheap here in the district, giving any needy person a bath or fresh meal whenever he could.

He was a good man, which was why he was part of Finley's system to keep track of the people who lived here.

Finley arrived on Planet Garwick at the young age of seven after losing both her parents in the rush to get on the ships. She couldn't remember any of the journey, or her life before that moment, apart from the few nightmares that plagued her.

According to Margaret, or Mag as Finley liked to call her, the oldest member of their community, the people at the bottom of the ship had found her unconscious, still clutching the bag that her mother had handed her. According to them, she'd stayed unconscious for the entire journey and even after arriving. When she finally awoken, she had no memory of who she was or what had happened.

Margaret had taken it upon herself to raise her, especially after losing her own son in the rush when he was just fourteen. But even though Finley had lived with Margaret while growing up, the whole community had been like family to her.

Together, they taught her how to read and write, math and science, and how to survive in this strange new world. Over the years, she slowly began to remember parts of who she was and where she'd come from, her name at first, and then the smell of her father's clothes and her mother's smile. Enough to know that she had once been someone before she came here. But not enough to fill the black hole that resided in her chest, aching for a past she couldn't quite recall.

Once she had taken a few turns through the maze of streets and alleys in the district, she made it to the highest street of the Hopeless District, which ran along the slow-moving canal—nicknamed "Blackwater Street" after the dark waters. It was much narrower here, and much dirtier, but odd stalls lined both sides of the water, built from bits of tarp and garbage bags. Each booth was run by the homeless or poor, trading whatever ware or service they could muster instead of selling for money. Money had little use in a place like this when no one had much of it.

Here, people were already roaming around, moving slowly from stall to stall, greeting friends and haggling for goods. It was in places like this that Finley forgot that her community was missing anything at all.

She walked swiftly down the street, waving and smiling at those who noticed her, counting the heads she recognized and mentally collecting those she didn't.

Even after living here for sixteen years and being practically raised by everyone in the community, faces still popped up that Finley didn't recognize. Whether they were newly fallen from the precarious position of the rich, or simply someone she had yet to come across, she always made sure to welcome them as the others had welcomed her.

She'd decided a long time ago that she wanted to give back to the people who helped raised her and protected her when they didn't need to, and while she couldn't fix their poverty or clean their homes, she could offer them protection.

And so, that's what she had become, a protector and keeper of the poor. Some called her "Hood," after Robin Hood—a fable character from the old world who had also protected the poor—and though she didn't recognize the tale, she was happy that she had a functioning place amongst them. Her job was to keep track of people, which was harder than she initially thought, especially with many of them not having permanent homes.

And because no one ever seemed to pay attention to them, not the rich nor the police, her people always managed to go missing. Whether they died from natural causes like starvation or exposure to the virus, or got caught stealing and were shot on sight. It was Finley's job to help them wherever she could, and make sure no one was forgotten.

She was halfway down the street when she stopped and turned into one of the large, cavernous openings to the abandoned brick warehouses that lined the canal. The doors were on the other side, but many had been kicked in from the street to allow for easier access. In this particular building, a few lucky people had built semi-permanent shelters.

It was sad what was considered shelter in this area. Here, they were lucky enough to have used sticks and newspapers to create partitions and roofs to small cordoned-off areas. Each one was designed in whatever way the occupant had known how to, with many simply being a fire pit and straw bed.

The one she was looking for, however, was slightly

different. Moving her hand to her jacket pocket, she touched the piece of paper that resided there, reminding herself of the task at hand. There was only one person she knew who could read cryo glyphs, a complicated scientific language that had been developed from some of the native languages of Garwick.

Her name was Jennifer Rose, and she'd been here nearly as long as Finley had. She'd come to Garwick as the daughter of a wealthy scientist at the age of fourteen, practically a genius. But during the hard years of establishment, her father died, and since all inheritance went to the governing body, she was left with nothing —no family nor home.

She'd long since grown out of being the preppy young woman she'd started life as, becoming a sarcastic streetwise brawler who didn't quite know when to shut her mouth instead. But she'd been one of the closest to Finley in age, and they'd grown up as friends.

They had helped each other out of trouble more times than she could count, and Jenny was probably the closest thing she'd ever have to a sister.

Jenny ran a small collection stall from her home in the Blackwater slums, reinventing things from the piles of trash she found at the dump. Finley told her on more than one occasion that she was too reckless, risking her life every time she went outside the wall to visit the places where no one else dared to go, but she ignored her every time. And while she worried about Jenny, she had to admit that if she could trust anyone to look after themselves, it would be her.

She was more likely to shank a person than hug them on the best of days. And to this day, she was still as sharp as a whip, her amazing mind retaining every-thing she had ever learned. If anyone could read the cryo glyphs, it would be her.

When Finley made it to the back of the warehouse where Jenny's home resided, she slowed, the hairs on the back of her neck prickling. She halted, ears straining. Stillness fell upon her, and nothing moved, except for the steady *whoosh* of the canal and bits of tarp moving in the constant breeze. It was so quiet, almost too quiet…

Heart seizing, she jogged over to the entrance of Jenny's stall, the tarp curtains hanging closed. It was early; a lot of people would still be asleep or out getting supplies in the safety of the horizon light. But Jenny was an early riser, and she was always creating some-thing out of nothing.

Finley couldn't remember a time when she had come in here and couldn't hear the sound of Jenny tinkering away, melding trash into something amazing and new.

She held her breath as she went to lift the curtain away, but a part of her already knew what she would find.

There were stuff strewn everywhere, bits of metal and plastic littering her normally tidy space. The fire pit in the center had been left long enough to sink into embers, and there was no sign of her friend anywhere.

Chest contracting, she carefully analyzed the space. Perhaps Jenny had left in a hurry for an emergency or birth—as she often helped the midwives deliver newborn babies into the community. But Finley had never known her to leave her space in such a mess. She never could leave anything in the wrong place—an issue she carried over from the old world.

No, what her space told Finley was that someone else had been here, or she had been removed forcibly. It was unlikely that she'd been kidnapped; the area was too haphazard for someone to just snatch her. With her space so chaotic, she'd have had to have put up a fight, and others would've heard or seen something. Someone would've come to fetch Finley, and she'd have already been looking.

It was more likely that she didn't come back since the last time she started the fire, and it was impossible that she'd send someone to her home to retrieve something, as she never trusted anyone else in her space. Finley tried to calm her breathing. It was no use panicking; she knew she had to think logically.

If Jenny had been taken, Finley didn't want to cause an upset. The citizens here usually got aggressive when they panicked, and she didn't want anyone to get killed by the police for rioting. But she also knew she had to track her friend down.

Quietly surveying Jenny's home again, Finley tried to look for any sign of where her friend could have gone, but she came up short. Her weapons were gone, but nearly everyone in the Hopeless District carried a knife or some other form of weapon, so it wasn't unusual for Jenny to have left armed.

Gritting her teeth, she pulled out the note and scanned it again, huffing when she still couldn't decipher any clues from it. She shoved it in her pocket aggressively before turning and marching out of Jenny's home and the warehouse altogether, letting the humid canal air clear her lungs and her mind.

She needed to stay calm and think this through. She had to if she wanted to find Jenny. She'd check her friend's usual rendezvous and ask around before jumping to the worst conclusion. But despite her stubborn optimism, a small voice couldn't help but whisper to Finley that something bad was afoot, and her friend was caught in the middle of it.

CHAPTER
THREE

F inley was on her way out of the third and final location that Jenny usually hung around when she started to panic. Sure, she was a badass and spent most of her time separating fights over territory and sneaking around the cops, but it was rare that she ever seriously lost someone so young to anything other than a tragic accident. Heart racing, she began the jog back to her place, planning to regroup and think of a plan.

Just as she was about to turn back onto the boulevard, she ran into John Masterson, a close friend of

Jenny's. Hope sparking, she ran straight up to him. He didn't see her at first, his face a mask of what looked like concentration, and he jumped slightly when she touched his shoulder.

"Oh! Hood, I didn't see you there." He smiled sheepishly.

Normally, Finley would laugh and stop for a casual conversation, but her mind was far too frazzled. "I can't stop for long, John. I was just wondering if—" She was cut off from her question when she noticed his expression change again, and she realized it was pain. "John? Is everything okay?"

He lifted his hand to his mouth before speaking. "No, actually. I think I need to see a doctor. There's a sharp pain in my teeth."

"Have you been drinking too much of the sweet stuff again?" John had an appetite for sweet things, specifically the homebrewed blackberry mead he drank more of himself than he sold.

"You'd think so, but I haven't touched the stuff since last month. I haven't been feeling good enough to drink even that," he explained.

Finley frowned and tried to think of how to help him. She was worried about Jenny, but she still cared for everyone else on these streets. "Do you remember what might have caused it? What were you doing when it started?"

He looked puzzled for a minute, obviously thinking, before recognition sparked in his eyes.

"I went and got the vaccine with Jenny! A week after, I started feeling queasy," he answered.

Her heart sank at his words. That bloody vaccine!

The state had been pushing everyone to get the new vaccine, practically shoving it down their throat. Usually, they paid no attention to what the people in the Hopeless District did, but recently, they'd been targeting them more and more, and a lot of vulnerable people had caved to their persuasion.

It wasn't even that Finley was against the idea of a vaccine. If she trusted it, she'd have been the first in line to get it, to protect her community, but something just felt off about it. The state kept parroting on about how people hadn't taken anything seriously in the old world, and that was why it became such a problem, and the humans had to leave, but she wasn't quite sure what they were even vaccinating them against. No one had gotten ill and turned into an Antiqua in years, so why the sudden rush?

She'd been telling anyone who'd listen not to take it until they knew more about it, but even with her popularity and known presence, she couldn't reach everyone. And she'd been especially shocked when, last month, Jenny said she was going with some others to get it. Together, she and Finley had been some of the most critical of the shot, and Jenny was the last person she'd have ever expected to cave.

But Jenny had fallen in with a different crowd recently, the vigilantes who thought they were going to fix the inequality that Roseallan City was built upon. Life was hard enough already for the people here, and these rebels liked to prey on the weak, just as the state did. They convinced people that it was worth risking their lives for a bigger cause, but in Finley's mind, dead was dead, revolution or not.

After a few weeks of the chip being implanted, Finley assumed that everything was going to be smooth sailing, but now she wasn't so sure.

Now her chest filled with fear and anxiety. People had to go back to the medical center if they started feeling ill in any way. If John was feeling sick, then maybe Jenny had also felt unwell and headed back to the center for medical care. That might explain why her place was such a mess.

Mind set on her next step, Finley put a firm hand on John's shoulder. "John, go to Jenny's place and tidy up a bit. Lie down and rest. I don't want you going anywhere, and I'll be back later this evening to check up on you," she said.

John nodded obediently, and she flashed him a smile before jogging off again, heading up onto the main boulevard and toward her apartment. But instead of going inside, she went over to where her bike was covered with a tarp.

As her most prized possession, Finley looked after her baby well. And while she knew that no one from the district would steal from her—they all knew her too well—she wouldn't put it past the cops to think that she'd stolen it or something.

She smiled as she did every time she uncovered her crimson beauty, her metalwork shining in the dim winter sunlight. Beautiful. Slipping her helmet on, she mounted her feet and started up the engine, loving the way it purred to life beneath her hands. She had spent most of her younger years saving up for the bike, and it had taken nearly everything she had.

She first saw someone riding the model back when

she was just thirteen, when it was still the newest model on the marker, during a brief trip to uptown to collect some dumped furniture. She still remembered gasping as the man turned it on, the engine roaring. A shiver ran up her spine, and as he pulled away smoothly and accelerated rapidly, she knew she needed one for herself.

Finley had been realistic, though. She knew she needed somewhere decent to live first if she wanted to keep her own bike in good condition, so she started taking on jobs in the shops uptown, hiring herself out for deliveries and odd jobs. She learned a lot of skills on the streets, along with how to fix a lot of things—since nothing she got ever really came new.

It had taken her until she was eighteen, but she eventually managed to buy an apartment—completely rundown with nothing working—and fix it up. Then she rented it out to a few struggling students until she was twenty-two, when she could finally afford to buy her beauty and move into her own home. It had been hard living on the streets for so long, knowing that there was a half-decent shelter somewhere that she owned. But now that she finally had her bike with her, she knew it had all been worth it.

Peeling away from the alley, she made her way onto the road, quickly moving from the run-down buildings that marked the district into the slightly better-kept area of midtown—home to those who were just able to get by without much struggle. Roseallan City was designed in rings, with the wealthiest of the wealthiest living at the very center—safe from the threat of the Antiqua. The further the ring spread out, the rougher it got, but it also meant that those living in destitute far outnumbered those with wealth.

Sometimes it baffled her how so few people could rule over so many, simply with something as conceptual as money.

As the road quality grew better, and the streets grew cleaner, Finley made her way over to the medical center. There were plenty of large, bright signs, thanks to all the pro-vaccine propaganda the city was pushing. But regardless, she knew her way. Finley knew practically every corner of the city, both the upper parts and the underground sewers. The only sections that had managed to remain a mystery to her were the homes and buildings of the ultra-rich. They could smell her poverty from a mile away, and they were more likely to shoot her on sight than offer her a tour of their sparkling homes.

But she pushed the bitterness away as she pulled into the sterile white building that housed the medical center. There were rows of people lined outside, and several officers in black uniforms kept the crowd orderly and quiet. They glanced at her as she pulled up, the old model of her bike telling them that she wasn't wealthy. However, the fairly decent quality was able to disguise the fact that she was from the dregs.

After a terse observation, the officers all turned back to their positions, and Finley released a tense breath. The cops here were jumpy, more trouble than they were worth. Law enforcement here wasn't like how it used to be in the old world; they only seemed to serve those who had the money to pay for them. Which meant that it was often her own people who were staring down the wrong side of their guns.

She jogged up to the entrance, skipping the line and giving the officers a wide grin. A smiling woman in green scrubs looked over at her as she stepped up.

"Ma'am, I have to ask you to wait in line if you wa—"

"I'm not here for the vaccine." She cut her off, eager to move on from this place as quickly as she could. "I'm looking for a friend. She got the vaccine last month, and I need to know if she's here or at the hospital."

The woman frowned and forced herself to keep her plastic smile on her face. "Ma'am, I strongly advise that you get the vaccine—"

"Her name is Jennifer Rose. Just tell me if she's here or not!" Finley snapped, surprised at how thin her patience was growing.

The woman looked shocked, but she nodded her head and hurried inside. Finley tapped her foot impatiently as she watched the woman speak to several more scrub-wearing minions and look down at a tablet.

When the woman came back fifteen minutes later, Finley's mood had darkened completely, and she scowled hard enough that the woman shook lightly as she stepped over.

"I'm sorry, ma'am, but we have no record of that person in the system."

She clenched her fists in frustration and gritted out, "Does that mean just here… or everywhere?"

"Everywhere, ma'am. We checked the database, and there's no record of her coming in for the vaccine."

"I know she did. I have a friend who came here with her!"

"I don't know what to tell you, but she's not—"

"Well, check again!" Finley shouted, her temper at its peak and her panic intensifying. The woman jumped and backed up a step, but before Finley could de-escalate the situation, one of the officers stepped in between them.

"Is there a problem here, doctor?" he asked the woman, not bothering to hide his sneer toward Finley. The doctor started to speak, but before she could, the officer turned toward Finley, his stance aggressive. "I'm going to need you to leave now."

"But—" Finley started.

"Move, or I will move you," he barked, and she grimaced at him. He went to reach for her, but she shook him off, stomping away.

She got back on her bike quickly, not willing to risk getting thrown in some dungeon or cell, but she did glare at them as she drove away, revving her engine more than she needed to. It wasn't until she started driving back downtown when she realized that she wasn't even back to square one. She was even more clueless than before.

She hadn't found Jenny, and what's worse, the people at the medical center didn't seem to have any record of her. Sure, Jenny could've used another name, but she had no need to. It wasn't like she was undercover. If anything, there was only a benefit to using her real name; a vaccine pass would allow her to access the shelters in midtown.

At the end of her tether, Finley pulled in rapidly,

spotting a tavern at the edge of the district, rough enough that she wouldn't feel out of place inside, but far enough from her home that it was unlikely for her to run into any of her usual crowd. She was in a terrible mood, too angry to talk to anyone, and she wasn't sure if she should let anyone know about Jenny yet. She'd never encountered this problem before.

She let the familiar smells of the tavern encircle her as she stepped into its dim light, the cavernous space full of raucous voices and laughter. Quietly, she walked up toward the bar, hoping to snag herself a strong remedy before retreating to one of the private booths at the back, so she could drink away her bad mood and clear her mind enough to think. But when she finally got to the bar, a large group of men shoved their way in front of her, pushing her so hard that she nearly stumbled and fell.

Immediately, her chest warmed with rage, her temper sparking like dry kindling. The loudest of the men, the thug who had pushed her and seemed to be their leader, didn't see her until she was only mere centimeters from him, her nails digging into his scalp as she grabbed hold of his greasy hair.

With a yank, Finley pulled him back, his spine bowing, leaving his neck vulnerable and exposed. He shouted at her, arms spinning, trying to grab onto her or anything to help him keep his balance. His friends seemed to have the mindset that they could take her, as all their faces twisted with anger and their voices rose. Without so much as a whisper, she pulled out the long knife that she kept on her at all times. They all went silent, including the rat that she had in her arms, as the cold steel kissed his skin.

Pulling his ear up to her mouth, she whispered menacingly. "Now, now," she tutted condescendingly, "what's the rush?"

His eyes bulged out of his skull as she applied pressure, and he rushed to answer her. At this point, the entire tavern had gone quiet, enthralled by the show happening at the bar.

"I-I don't know what you mean!" he balked.

"Really?" She gasped in mock surprise. "Surely, there must've been something you were in a hurry for, because if not," she jostled him even closer and inserted as much venom as she could into her voice, "then there was no reason for you to be so rude when you pushed me out of your way."

His friends moved nervously, keen to intervene but held still by her blade against their friend's neck. Growing tired of it all, Finley twisted the man in place, knocking him down so he knelt before her, her blade still at his jugular. "And there's nothing I hate more than needlessly obnoxious people!"

Exhausted, Finley was about to let him go when the man's face crumpled. "Sorry, please!" he yelled. "We *were* going somewhere; you were right!"

"Boss!" Several of his friends screamed out in protest, but she shook the man's shoulder threateningly, and they quickly silenced themselves.

"We were… well, you see—" he stuttered.

"Spit it out!"

"A rally! We were on our way to a rally. It's being

run by the Core over at the market center in mid-district."

She looked at him for a moment, her mind slowly mulling over this new information—unexpected, but helpful, nonetheless. "This the truth?" she asked quietly, her facial expression a non-believer.

He nodded rapidly. "Yeah, please, it is! Believe me!"

His friends began to get antsy as she watched him for a moment longer, enjoying the way he squirmed. They called out, echoing his confirmation of the truth, and when she was finally convinced, Finley dropped him onto the ground, causing a loud thud as his face hit the solid wooden floor.

She didn't look back as she stormed her way out of the tavern, ignoring the jeers and shouts. She still had to find Jenny, and now, she had a new lead to follow.

CHAPTER
FOUR

It was another Friday evening, and with the setting sun, came the usual unrest. It was always the same; people worked all week, throwing their backs out and putting all their energy into earning a less-than-decent wage for their families, and at the end of it all, when they were drained and realized, once again, how little all that effort gave them, they turned to the streets. At this point, it was like clockwork, the same problem but with different faces.

And it wasn't that Kingsley Bishop didn't sympathize with their plight. If it were up to him, he would've given them all the food and shelter they needed to get by, regardless of what their jobs were. It seemed only fair to him that everyone was given an equal footing in life.

But this endless rioting and rallying, all it did was upset the rich men and women who sat up in their ivory towers. And the more these people irritated them, the less they appeared as a useful asset. He worried that, one of these days, they would decide that the people were more of a burden than they were worth.

Only a fool could live in their world and not see it for what it really was—a factory. And if it wasn't yielding a profit, then the people above were ready to cut and run at a moment's notice. It was brutal, but it was the world that he had grown up in.

"Kingsley, Strage wants you down at the market square in mid-district. There's another rally going on," the mechanical voice that came through his communication system and straight into his ear robotically said to him. He grunted a non-verbal response into his mic and continued his route, not mentioning to his teammate that he was already on his way.

Jason Strage, the leader of the Scouts, was a hard son-of-a-bitch, and a narcissist at the best of times. Kingsley had learned pretty quickly that Strage couldn't be trusted to calm the people without the majority of them ending up dead or injured. He tried his best to be there when he could, to keep the people from Strage's grasp, but there was only so much he could do when Jason practically ran his life. If he didn't want Kingsley around, he could keep him away. And that thought scared him like no other.

Kingsley covered ground quickly, having long abandoned the street and resorting to jumping across the uniform roofs of the buildings that populated Roseallan City. The overpopulation of the city caused most of its unrest, but it meant that there were enough flat-topped slums and buildings to make for easy passage over the skyline. And as one of the cities "unfavorable" sections, it created a route that was less likely to result in major consequences for him.

That was the thing about working exclusively for the rich and famous in the only city left in human existence; over half the population hated him. Maybe not him specifically, but what he stood for.

Kingsley and his brethren soldiers were known as the "warriors for the just and right." But in truth? They were nothing more than mercenaries, hiding in the shadows and killing people like they were the right hand of God himself. It made him queasy just thinking about it all, but in the end, it was all he had. It was all he had ever known. This wasn't the old world, where he could've just cut ties and run, start over fresh somewhere else. No, here, he was trapped inside this wall, just like everyone else was. There was nowhere to go, nowhere to hide, and he was a slave to the unknown.

It took him less than ten minutes to cover half the city, slipping from the safety of the rooftops and down onto the wet pavement of mid-district. He could hear the chanting already, feeling their anger in the air like a rough caress, the static making his hair stand on end. He merged with the outer members of the crowd, becoming invisible amongst them, their bodies cloying and close but never touching his black leather-clad skin.

It was how it had always been, drowning amongst people, but forever separated from them. Pushing down the memories in his mind that tried to crawl their way to the forefront, he focused on the task at hand—what he could do to make this a semi-noble defeat for the people around him.

Because in the end, they would lose. They had lost the second they boarded those ships and followed their captors right into their new cage under the false guise of being saved.

When screams started to break out, now infused with terror rather than fury, Kingsley knew that his teammates had made their move. They always arrived at these rallies with a bang, using shock to do most of the work for them. He knew instantly that someone was already dead, their lifeblood likely pooling out onto the dirty cobblestone beneath them.

He pushed through the crowd with more vigor now, cutting through them like a boat through water. It became easier as the tide of people turned and began to run against him, desperate to flee what they quickly realized was a slaughter. It wasn't too long before there were only a few stragglers left, the ones foolish enough to fight.

He'd respect them—maybe even envy them—for standing up for themselves, but as all rallies that had come before, the people of the slums usually never stood a chance. The rich would never let go of their domination over the people of Roseallan City.

When a stocky man came at him, noticing that his

uniform match the ones of those brutalizing his friends, Kingsley slipped past his thrown fist effortlessly. Using the speed his lithely, muscled frame afforded him, Kingsley placed a calculated strike to the back of the man's neck. The stocky man dropped like a rock, his body heaping on the floor, but he was still alive and breathing. He would wake up, nothing more than a bruise to his pride and neck, and live another day to suffer alongside his friends and family.

Kingsley repeated this again and again as the other men notice how quickly he took down their comrades, hoping to take out what they saw as a great threat.

Suddenly, Kingsley froze in his rhythmic punches and swings when heard the piercing wail of a young girl, his blood going cold as memories tried to swarm his awareness. He had heard a scream like that before, seen the fright in her eyes as she scrambled to get away from the cause of her horror.

Him. It was him who had shocked her, who had her fleeing with tears running down her cheeks. She'd always looked at Kingsley with hope, with affection, and it had warmed a part of him that had begun to freeze over under the sole care of his heartless father. She had been his light, his love, and he'd been the reason that she died.

Wrenching his mind from the flashback that tried to envelop him, Kingsley ran toward the sound, covering himself in so much tension that he swore turned his body numb. But he needed to keep going if he was going to save the little girl whom he had failed to save so long ago…

He spotted Strage quickly, his hulking form too easy

to pick out amongst the smaller and more emaciated bodies of the poor. More bodies than he could count surrounded the man, their necks twisted and blood pouring from places that he knew were fatal. So many were dead already, but Kingsley knew that if he didn't do anything, the young girl and her mother would be next.

Kingsley calculated his situation quickly. He needed a way to divert Strage's attention without engaging him directly. If Strage found out that Kingsley wanted to save the mother and child, he'd likely kill them out of spite.

Strage had been suspicious of Kingsley from day one, jealous of the fact that his blood came from what others considered "purer stock." Kingsley never cared, hating the blood that flowed through his veins as much as he hated his father, but Strage had taken that carelessness for disdain and made it his life's goal to terrorize him.

Kingsley didn't care what happened to him, as long as it didn't affect anyone else. He could suffer—he deserved it for so many of his sins—but he refused to let anyone else die because of him. It was why he kept himself so isolated now. So, no one could be a target, and no one could get hurt.

Noticing several men still strong enough to hold their own in a fight, Kingsley headed toward them, using large and imposing movements to engage their fear receptors. As he had seen a hundred times, they formed a tightly-knit group but then backed away, bodies crouched low and defensive. He volleyed their hits easily, making sure to take a few and huff out of breath to keep their confidence high. Within minutes, he had them backing into Strage unwittingly, forcing the mercenary to abandon his post and focus on the bodies that had fallen upon him.

In the chaos, Kingsley skirted around them, stepping up quickly and quietly to the mother and her child. She flinched away from his gloved hand, and though it might have stung at one point, he now accepted it as his truth. Proof of his irredeemable soul.

Silently and gently, he firmly took her arm, ignoring the way her struggles pulled at his heart. When he pushed her toward the opening of an alleyway, she yanked her limb from him as if he had burnt her, grabbing at her child to protect her from what she considered to be a monster. She was right, too. Kingsley was no better than his brothers and sisters behind him, smiling at the chaos and the carnage.

He was about to turn to disengage the men still fighting with Strage when Ivan Richards—the nasty little snot who followed Strage around like he was some sort of second coming—grabbed his arm and shoved him hard against the brick wall of a building.

Kingsley's head snapped against the rough surface, drawing blood, but he kept his expression blank, affording the man nothing but a blank gaze.

"Ah, ah, ah," he tutted at Kingsley, grinning like a cat who had cornered the mouse. "I saw that little stunt," he hissed.

"I don't know what you're talking about," Kingsley spoke blankly, knowing it was his lack of emotion that would cut Ivan the most.

Teeth pulled back in a predicted snarl, Ivan called

out to Strage, fearful that if he didn't, he'd receive nothing but disapproval from their Scout leader.

"Strage! I caught our little boy here letting your playthings go!"

Strage broke from his battle immediately, his heavy body freezing far too quickly for the momentum he had seemingly built up. Kingsley always felt that the way he moved was unnatural, slightly too fast, slightly too strong, and that black look in his eyes was nothing short of demonic. He might have suspected some sort of possession if his own eyes didn't share a similar darkness, though his were frigid where Strage's burned.

Strage said nothing as he walked over, the men he was fighting with fleeing for their lives. He had been playing with them as he had intended to play with the mother and daughter duo, pushing them around, making them unable to run but also not killing them right away. It was cruel, and something Kingsley despised more than anything.

He had killed, yes. Kingsley was just as much a murderer as Strage and Richards. But at least he gave them swift deaths; he didn't play with his food as they did.

"Now why'd you have to go and do that?" Strage demanded, his devious grin contradicting the seriousness in his voice. He was happy that Kingsley had messed up, because the one thing Strage liked more than killing was punishing him.

"Wait!" A clear female voice called out, and Kingsley immediately knew who it was before she stepped up to the trio. Ruby Thompson, a fellow mercenary.

Kingsley wanted to growl at her to get away. She had no business getting involved in his problems, but Ruby had always been like this. Maybe one of the only other mercenaries here who hated her kin as much as he did and didn't take any joy from anarchy and death. If he had been in the business of making friends, she'd have been one of them. Despite Kingsley's cold, dismissive nature, Ruby had been nothing but loyal and supportive. Always standing up for him whenever she could. But that's exactly what he didn't want.

He didn't want people being there for him, caring for him. He had lost that privilege a long time ago. With her. With his love. And now he swallowed every punch, every cut, and every scar that fate brought his way because, in the end, he couldn't protect the one who had meant the most to him. And now, because of that, she was dead, and here he was, doing a whole load of nothing with his life.

"Stay out of this, Ruby!" He grimaced, ignoring the alarming look that raised her perfect black brows moments before the first punch landed hard on his right cheek.

CHAPTER
FIVE

It had taken Finley mere minutes to ride her bike down to the market center in mid-district, her machine moving swiftly and precisely through the alleys that formed the main roads. But now that she was here, she was regretting not having that drink.

The riot, or "rally" as they tried to call it, was being run by the Core, an anonymous rebel group that claimed to be working for her people—the poor and the unfortunate. It was the same crowd that Jenny had fallen in with a few months ago, and now she was missing.

Finley might not be the sharpest tool in the shed, but a hammer could still do a fuck ton of damage, and she couldn't see how this could be just a coincidence. The rebels liked to go under the disguise of being martyrs, appealing to those who were tired and upset. But in the end, all they did was create unrest, death, and harsher punishments for the poor buggers who were left behind.

If a revolution was achievable, Finley would be the first to champion it. But the sad truth was that they were stuck here, and not even a miracle was going to turn things around. Most days, it's better to just avoid drawing attention as much as possible.

But when she arrived to the market square, Finley found nothing but anarchy. The mercenaries that the state hired for "behavioral management" had moved in by the time she'd gotten there, scaring the citizens away and punishing those who remained and fought. Her heart was pounding, worried that Jenny would be amongst them, but after combing through the leftover crowd, Finley was sure she wasn't here.

For a moment, she was relieved. If Jenny wasn't here, then she might still be safe, but a darker part of Finley's mind knew that it had been nearly twenty-four hours since she had discovered Jenny missing. It could've been longer even, considering that she hadn't seen her the day before either, and she knew that nothing good could come from her being unreachable for so long.

Finley was about to leave, to continue her search,

when she saw something that just couldn't be condoned—no matter how much of a pacifist she was. She spotted one of the mercenaries, one who seemed to have way too much fun killing as many people as he could, backing a mother and her small daughter into a corner. Immediately, Finley knew she had to stop whatever he was planning, a cruel smirk on his face telling her it was nothing good. But just before she could make her way over, standing still in the shadows of the buildings that allowed her some cursory cover, she hesitated.

There was a man, his dark hair and pale skin making him stand out against his tanner adversaries, backing a group of men toward the offending mercenary. He was obviously a mercenary himself; the uniform was unmistakable, but she sensed in his movements that he didn't have the same ominous intentions as his crewmates did. No, this man fought with surety, his movements firm and calculated, but he never gave a hit that wasn't manageable, and he made sure that the men he fought remained relatively unharmed.

Looking back at the men he had dropped, she realized they were some of the only ones still breathing, them and the victims of a dark-haired female mercenary who'd focused on stragglers. Finley tried to tell herself that a mercenary was a mercenary, and filled with shame that she had left the mother and child vulnerable while she played spectator to this bloody show, she went to protect them as she had originally intended.

But before she could even take a step forward, the two groups of men collided, the mercenary who'd been focused on the woman and child distracted by the more urgent danger. Finley expected to see them perform some sort of pincer effect, killing the men from both sides.

But instead, the unusual pale-skinned man broke from the pack, expertly slipping around them and to the woman and child. In unhurried but firm movements, he guided them both away, and within seconds, the risk to their lives was reduced to nearly none.

What happened next had taken her by surprise, more than she had anticipated, which was where she found herself now, gawking at the picture before her. The unusual mercenary was pinned up against the wall, his body relaxed despite the obvious threat to his life, by a fourth mercenary that Finley hadn't noticed yet— though, by the way he grinned at the larger mercenary with the cruel eyes, she suspected that he wasn't a kind man.

The dark-haired female approached the men quickly, her body telling Finley that she was worried, which was then confirmed by her shouted caution for the man. For a moment, Finley was strangely jealous of the female mercenary. She clearly knew the pale-skinned man; the concern on her face was nothing short of familiar, and the idea that this beautiful creature was so intimate with the pinned man irked Finley for some reason.

She'd had a few lovers in her life, a few men here and there who'd found her attractive, but overall, she was independent. She liked being free to move around as she liked, and she rarely formed deep romantic connections. People always seemed to be suffocating, and she could never bring herself to want to bring them into her life fully, to have them in her space day and night. The last time she had… she'd been too young to realize what it was. And now the nightmares haunted her every sleeping hour.

She could accept that this man was attractive. At closer inspection, his face was aristocratic and smooth, with high cheekbones and dark brows. Despite his unresponsive expression, his lips were lush, and she could only imagine what they would look like smiling, but smiling didn't seem like something he did much. His frame was tall and muscular, but not in the bulging and hulking way of the comrade whose fist had just slammed into his face. The sound of flesh impacting against flesh made her flinch, and she frowned at her own reaction.

Finley was no newcomer to aggression; it was pretty difficult to avoid when she lived in a world where fighting was necessary for survival. She was a seasoned pro as far as combat went, and she hadn't cringed at the sight of violence ever since she was a little girl. And even then, she had been mostly numbed to it.

But now, watching this brutal assault of two men against one, she wanted to shout—to cry out and stop them. The urge was so strong that she gasped, placing her hands over her mouth to stop the scream that tried to scratch its way from her throat.

She tensed her body against the waves of this urge to run forward and help him—protect him. The raven-haired woman looked like she was in pain, her face grimaced, but she also looked accepting of what was happening, and it made anger rise in Finley.

How could she just stand there and watch this happen, when the man in question had done nothing wrong? Maybe he had shown mercy where it wouldn't typically be shown by their order, but surely, that was no excuse for such brutal punishment!

She released a silent breath when the beating stopped, the men stopping as quickly as they'd started. Finley was too far away to hear their lowly exchange of words, but then the hulking one—most likely a leader by the way he carried himself and his seemingly unyielding authority—turned and moved quickly, more quickly than he should've been able to, out of the square and disappearing down a street.

Finley was about to leave, thinking this disaster was over and saving herself the trouble of getting caught, when the smaller man next to the prone form of the beaten mercenary began to beat him again.

At the sound of the man's ragged groans, she was unable to stop herself any longer; the need in her to protect others roared to life in aid of this seemingly defeated man. She began ripping into them before she, or anyone else, knew what she was doing, her hands flying with her nails hooked like claws. She raked her nails down the side of his cheek, drawing satisfying blood and successfully stealing his focus from the man.

Finley jumped back, her cognitive mind catching up with her actions and beginning to plan her next steps, leaving the lectures for herself later.

"You little bitch! I'm going to tear you from fucking limb to limb," the man spat, the words searing her ears and stoking the fire of her fury. She quietly pulled out the long blade from her boot, keeping it behind her thigh to conceal it.

She didn't allow herself time to reconsider; there

was no room for doubt in a fight like this. Their skills were likely matched, his from professional training and hers from sheer experience. One wrong hesitation, and she could end up dead, or worse, imprisoned. And that definitely wasn't where she was prepared to spend the night, rotting in one of their dank jail cells, awaiting an unfair trial that would likely end in her banishment from inside the wall and into the Antiqua-infested dunes.

The man threw a few deadly hits, and she dodged them, with just a few of them catching her arm and side, leaving stripes of fire on her skin. She kept herself from striking immediately like her instincts demanded, letting herself size him up completely, testing out his speed and agility. When she thought she had a handle on his parameters, she began to attack. He was quick, but he also lacked accuracy, made worse by his weakened left knee that definitely wasn't as strong as his right.

Using this small piece of information to her advantage, Finley fainted a right strike, spinning into his unprotected left side as he attempted to block a blow that never came. Instead, she slipped her blade into the soft part of his back, just beneath his rib cage, the knife likely piercing a kidney. Regardless, his gargled scream told her all she needed to know; he was incapacitated enough that she could make her escape.

Despite her own heroic complex, she hadn't come here today to commit a crime, and it was more important to her that she lived another day to find Jenny than waste another moment on this scumbag.

As soon as his body moved away from Finley's, his

brain instinctively moved him away from the source of his injury. She turned to make a run for it, but froze when she saw both the beaten man and the raven-haired woman staring at her. Their faces revealed nearly nothing, their expressions mostly serious, but the woman held some vestiges of softness within her brows, and Finley took the hint for what she hoped was a ticket to freedom. She sprinted past them, where the woman held the man upon her smaller shoulder, a breath whooshing from her chest when they didn't immediately reach out to stop her.

Without looking back, she worked her legs as fast as she could, taking turns down streets, relying more on instinct than on sight. In the back of her mind, she groaned at the reminder that she had left her prized bike behind at the square, but with luck on her side, she hoped that the bike would be safe for the night. Tomorrow, she would return, take it home, and continue her search on foot, making sure to keep a low profile.

She began to slow down only when the streets took on the familiar disuse of the Hopeless District, the old but maintained buildings falling into rubble and rot. She let herself pause, her breaths hard and panting, and her head still spun with the high of the adrenaline. It had been a stupid idea, fighting a mercenary, and Finley doubted that the man had deserved her defending him —he was part of their posse, after all.

She was just about to speed up again, resolving to go home and wash today's stress and anger off her body with a scalding shower, when a dark form thumped down in front of her, and her blood turned cold.

Before she knew what was happening, she found herself being pinned against the alley wall, the pressure of a heavier body squeezing all the air from her lungs. She cringed, fearing it was the mercenary she'd cut, coming back to fulfill his promise to gut her. But when nothing happened, she plucked up the courage to open her eyes. Her heart faltered in its steady beating at the blazing green eyes that met hers.

His face was bruised, the skin already swelling, but even that couldn't diminish his strikingly good looks. Even beaten, he made her skin tingle. His face was as blank as it had been back at the square, and it dawned on Finley now just how tall he was, with his head a good half a foot above hers that she had to strain her neck to look up at him. But before she could shove him back, scream at him to let her go, he spoke, and her heart seemed to stop altogether.

"Just what stupid thing was going through your head," he growled, his lips pulling back to show his straight white teeth. But all that was dimmed by the clanging of recognition in her brain.

She had heard that voice before, heard it echoing through her nightmares again and again, like the doomed tolling of a bell. It was higher pitched, belonging to a young boy at the time and full of pain and fear, but she could've recognized it anywhere. It was him; it was Kingsley Bishop, the son of the man who had killed her father…

And her first and only love.

CHAPTER
SIX

Finley grew flustered when she finally barged her way inside the back door of the food shelter that she worked part-time in. It wasn't a job she needed; she earned enough from the odd repair jobs she did, and the rest of what she needed were often given to her for free from the homeless people she protected, as a way of showing their gratitude.

But even a shelter like this had an entrance fee so the rich could get richer from the starvation of over half their citizens, not to mention the mandate in place that demanded for people to show a vaccine pass before they could enter any official government building. Some of the more sympathetic businesses were smart enough to ignore it, but too many of them had taken to the rule vehemently, including all the food banks and shelters.

Luckily, Finley managed to get herself a fake pass, stole one from a medical center back when the rule first came into play. Unfortunately, Finley couldn't steal enough for everyone. Otherwise, they would catch on to the deception and come up with some other way to stop her people from eating, so instead, she used her pass to get food to the people who couldn't get in.

Her head was reeling as she stumbled through the kitchen, hanging her jacket up with the other coats of the staff and numbly slipping on her apron.

She had seen… No. It couldn't be. He was gone. The boy she had loved all those years ago, the face she saw in her dreams and nightmares alike. It was from the past. A far and distant place where nothing could actually touch her.

But despite her denial, she couldn't shake away the certainty that it had been him. Older, yes, and colder, too. But those eyes, she'd know those eyes anywhere. Her body involuntarily shivered at the thought of his intense gaze and the memory of his gruff voice when he'd caught up to her.

"Speak, girl, or I'll make you, and I'm sure you won't like my method of persuasion."

That lit a fire under her, Finley's pride reacting to the threat, and she jumped to life. She struggled hard enough that he almost stumbled, but he redoubled his strength and kept her firmly plastered against the wall.

"I'm no girl," she spat, "and you're welcome for saving your ass."

He laughed humorlessly. "I didn't need saving."

It was her turn to scoff. "Oh, right, because getting beaten to death was on your list of things to do tonight. Sorry, next time, I'll be sure to leave you to die."

Her words were harsh, the rage and anxiety inside of her a potent cocktail that made her tongue sharp and her heart hard. Every second she looked at him, her mind began to reject what it thought it had recognized.

Yes, he looked like Kingsley, and most likely, it was him. But he was no longer the little boy she'd once loved. His cold face and biting words were not what she remembered of that gentle young man, and in his place, was a monster wearing his face. This was not her childhood friend, but the son of the man who had murdered her father in cold blood.

When his stares got to be too much, she tried kicking out at his leg, hoping to capitalize on his distraction. Unfortunately, his skills were much better than she had anticipated, considering the absolute defeat she had witnessed just moments ago.

"Do I... do I know you?" he asked quietly. Though his tone was hesitant, it was still chillingly bitter.

For a second, an urge rose in her chest, strong and moving, and it told her to tell him. To remind him of their years together, and the love they had shared even at such a young age. It was that naïve and hopeful part of her that still believed there was some good in the world. But she had meant what she said; she was a woman now, not a girl. And she knew very well that the world was a dark and dangerous place, and the man in front of her was more likely to slice her throat than welcome her with open arms.

This was no reunion, and she decided right then and there that he would never know who she was. If his father had killed hers, then she could be their next target. She doubted that they'd want the daughter and witness to their crime running around the city freely.

She sneered at him instead of answering his question. "If you're not going to kill me, then let me go. I have things to do."

He didn't reply, just kept glaring at Finley like her face had somehow offended him, and it was almost enough to make her blush.

She gritted her teeth at the urge, willing her body to be still and cold. She was about to make some other snide remark, when suddenly, he began pulling back. The loss of his warm, strong body holding up her own was a shock, and she almost fell from the loss of it. By the time she regained her balance, he was gone.

Which left her where she was now, at her evening job wondering if she had imagined the entire thing. Any part of her that could've been excited about this development had been snuffed out when she realized the danger he could pose to her if he found out her real identity. And she felt the strain of yet another stress falling upon her back like a boulder.

However, determined to not let his presence ruin her or the life she had built for herself, she tried to shake away her confusion. She had a mind that sought out mysteries like a bloodhound in search for food. Whenever she was faced with a puzzle, she couldn't help but want to solve it. It was both a curse and a blessing, and in this case, it was almost painful to force her mind to drop it.

When the bare necessities in life weren't promised, Finley got pretty good at shutting out any intrinsic needs. Hunger, thirst, things like that. She could fast for forty days and still remain strong. Her body was a tool that she had sharpened over years of experience, and she refused to be distracted by the appearance of some pretty little boy from a thousand years ago.

———

The next few hours at the shelter passed by quickly, with familiar faces gathering to receive the only decent meal they'd likely get all week. Finley tried to nod and converse with those she knew, and welcome those she didn't, but she could feel herself getting distracted. And when ten rolled around, she was exhausted from the effort it took not to think about everything that had happened.

The dining hall was bustling, but mostly with conversation as most of the meals had already been handed out for the night. She glanced down at her wristwatch and watched the arm tick toward the ten, a heavy breath leaving her chest. It was then that every-thing seemed to quiet for a moment. The air became still, and a strange tension rose, strong enough to make the hairs on the back of her neck prickle.

She was about to say something, ask those closest to her what was going on, when all of a sudden, the stillness broke. In its place, absolute chaos rained down. Bodies that had stopped only moments before broke into a torrent of movement, thrashing out at the people around them with the most horrid of screams.

Startled, she threw herself over the counter, trying to find the cause of the fight so she could break it up. But everywhere she looked, people were fighting, and those who weren't were fleeing as quickly as they could. No matter where she looked, she couldn't seem to find the epicenter of the disruption. It was as if everyone had suddenly gone feral, and when she managed to grab one of the men closest to her, she looked into his eyes and saw utter blackness.

Finley jumped when he started to attack her, and she pushed his body away as quickly as she could. But it was too late, and soon, there were at least five of them turning their attention onto her. Gulping, she crouched down into a fighting stance, trying not to think about how this was her second big fight in one day, and also trying not to let her confusion distract her from her survival. She didn't want to hurt any of these people, but it was obvious that something wrong was going on.

She deflected the first few people who came at her; they were aggressive but uncalculated, meaning that she could dodge a few of them. She tried not to listen to the sound of bodies dropping, tried not to look down onto the faces of people she knew and see the lifelessness that would be in their eyes. But eventually, the sheer number began to gain on her, and with six of them at every side, she couldn't move fast enough to protect herself.

Blows landed on both her sides, into the soft part of

her kidneys, winding her and tearing at her hair. She was sure that she was going to die, killed by those she loved and protected, when suddenly, all the bodies that had been hurling at her were gone.

She looked up, confused, and looked into the same pair of green eyes that she had seen earlier today. But these were different; they weren't cold and indifferent, but filled with… concern? Panic? And after a moment, she knew it was him. It was her Kingsley, and he had come to save her.

———

When Kingsley carried her over toward an empty alley, the woman was fuming, her gaze—which had been vulnerable only minutes before—turned into defensiveness. He didn't blame her; he had ambushed her earlier and been less than kind, after all. He hadn't really been aware of what he was doing except follow the inexplicable urge to go after her. To know who she was and where she was going.

He realized that she reminded him of the girl he had lost long ago and tried to pull away. But he hadn't been able to stop himself from thinking about her. Like an alcoholic who couldn't leave the bottle for too long, he followed this woman to a food shelter and watched intently, soaking up her movements and words like a sponge in water.

He was obsessed, but he didn't give a damn.

But when the fights broke out, he hadn't been able to stop himself from rushing in to protect her. She was feisty and skilled, reminding him of a fierce lioness protecting her cubs, and he'd been entranced by her ferocity. But even she couldn't win against the large feral crowd that had been taken over by madness. A madness his people had a hand in.

"What the fuck was that?!" the woman screeched, her eyes burning with fire, expelling an aura that Kingsley found so attractive.

"Something you shouldn't concern yourself with," he replied, trying to keep the edge out of his voice, obviously failing from the way the woman's temper was sparking in her eyes.

"Oh, no you don't!" she shouted again, her finger poking into his chest painfully, though Kingsley didn't react. "A government clone is not going to tell me where I can or can't go. Your benefits never apply to people like me, and as far as I'm concerned, neither do your stupid rules!"

With that, she began stomping down the alley that he had deposited her in, the one outside the shelter that had been overrun with angry citizens, and surprisingly, across the street from the woman's apartment building. He felt a strange warming in his chest and was puzzled. He thought he felt… angry?

The emotion was foreign to Kingsley. In this form, anyway. He was used to feeling disdain for his kin, hatred toward them and their plans, but this burning feeling in his chest was something that he hadn't experienced since he was a young boy.

"Where do you think you're going?" he growled, marching after her, heavy steps echoing in the alley.

"None of your damn business!" she shouted back. And when he grabbed her arm, she spun around, an expression on her face that looked like she wanted to kill him.

"No, not if you're going to get yourself killed!"

"Why do you care?"

Kingsley was taken aback by her question. Why *did* he care? He didn't know, and it was bothering him how he was being moved by feelings and urges he long thought he'd killed in himself. Unable to come up with an answer, he simply stared at the small woman next to him, at her frazzled hair and clean leather clothes. Her style contradicted with what he knew about her, that she was one step away from being homeless, and that her people lived in the poorest parts of this city. He should feel nothing for this woman, similar to how he felt nothing for all the other poor suckers he often came across, and yet, he found himself wanting to protect her.

"Please, not now. Don't go out tonight," he pleaded, his voice as close to a beg as he had ever gotten. She stared at him, her eyes hard, a stubborn tilt to her chin.

"Why?" she simply asked.

But Kingsley said nothing, imploring her with his eyes. They stared at each other for so long that he was sure she was about to toss his grip off again, when suddenly, a tension cracked in her posture, and a strange vein of relief pooled through him.

"Fine, but you have a lot of explaining to do."

He tried not to let her tone bug him. He was in control here, and he wouldn't give it up for something that didn't benefit him.

Why, then, did he feel in danger of spilling all his secrets?

CHAPTER
SEVEN

Morning came all too swiftly for Finley, and with it, a nervous doubt. It had been over twenty-four hours since Jenny had gone missing, and it was time to start being realistic about what could've happened to her. She got dressed quietly in the early morning light and could almost imagine that it was another normal day.

If it had been, she would've moved from her bed and into the kitchen, still in her pajamas, where she would've likely taken a good hour or so enjoying her breakfast. She didn't usually give herself time off, but Finley always liked to spend Monday mornings taking things a bit slower.

Then, when she had eaten her cereal and read a chapter of her newest book, she would've showered, allowing herself those extra five minutes under its warm spray before getting dressed and leaving for some casual calls with the people on the streets.

Instead, today she felt the weight of dread that pressed against her. Her actions were quick and routine, and there was no trace of her relaxing morning in sight. She didn't even have the heart to startle when she moved into her kitchen and found Kingsley sitting on her small, second-hand sofa. The sight might've even made her laugh on some other day, his large body balancing precariously on the flimsy furniture, and his normally composed expression groggy from the lack of sleep.

Instead, she said, "You're still here."

"That's what I promised," he replied blankly, and Finley gulped at the sound of his voice, husky from whatever sleep he'd managed to get.

"Okay, then start talking," she ordered.

She was still slightly mad at herself for letting him strongarm her last night. She had been so angry when she realized that he'd taken her away from the people she was meant to protect, which had only morphed into terror when she realized he now knew where she lived. And she let that fear curb her need to return to the source of the issue, to go to bed and sleep when her friends and family were out there being slaughtered.

If his explanations were as good, she was sure she

might just about stab him; the past relationship be damned.

"It's... complicated," he muttered, and she rolled her eyes so hard they might've seen her brain.

"Said everyone, ever."

He sighed. "What happened last night... It's going to happen again. And again, and again." He looked hurt as he spoke, but Finley struggled to muster any sympathy when everything he'd told her was vague and unspecific.

"Okay," she said slowly, "but why? What's causing it?"

"I can't tell you."

She clenched her jaw so hard she thought her teeth might break. "Why?"

He didn't meet her eyes when he said, "Because it wouldn't change the outcome."

"What? Are we all going to die or something?! Come on, Kingsley, spit it out! I gave you a chance last night, and now you're here preaching some martyr bullshit?! No! You need to tell me what's going on!"

"It won't change anything. The vaccine—wait," he paused, and his eyes flew to meet hers. If her own mind hadn't been spinning with the words that he had nearly said, she might've realized her mistake. "How... how do you know my name?"

"You told me. Last night," she tried to say flippantly, which was hard when she wasn't really concentrating. "Is this about the vaccine? That's what you were about to say, wasn't it? I... I fucking knew it!"

"No, wait. Stop! Stop right now. You don't know

what I was about to say, and I know I didn't tell you my name last night. I don't even know yours."

"I'm not an idiot. You can drop the lie, ninja boy. Considering the beating you took yesterday, I don't think your mind is very reliable."

They both stood there, Kingsley filled with agitation, staring at each other. They were in a stalemate, both having revealed cards that they hadn't wanted to. Do they keep pushing? Risk revealing information they both wanted behind doors?

It was Finley who looked away first. She trusted her intuition enough to not push for more answers, and she needed to remember that this man wasn't the boy she once knew, who would've hugged her and told her that everything was okay. No, this man, the one who stood in front of her, rigid and tense, could kill her if he wanted to. And with the information she had just uncovered, she realized she had a lot more to do.

She didn't know what was happening, but she knew it had something to do with the vaccine, and she would bet everything she had that Jenny was somehow in the middle of it.

Finley spun around and grabbed her knife from the side, sliding it into her thigh holster and walking over to the door, opening it, and raising an eyebrow at Kingsley, indicating for him to leave. He stood up and walked toward her, his figure imposing, but she held his gaze as he walked out the door, and she shut it behind them.

In the alley, he asked her, "Where are you going?"

"The morgue," she replied without taking her eyes off the area around them, her heart sinking when she remembered that her bike was still at the square in mid-district.

When she did meet Kingsley's inquisitive gaze, she couldn't help but say, "I have a friend who went missing. It's the last place I haven't checked."

She tried to keep her tone nonchalant, but she knew a part of her sorrow was seeping into her voice. A part of her hoped she would find her friend there, peacefully at rest having died from something quick and simple, but the more she dug into this mystery, the more she was beginning to realize that something bigger was in motion.

For a second, she swore he looked regretful, a pain so vast and endless filling his gaze, but it was gone before she could fully register it. Dropping behind his mask of apathy so surely, she was half convinced that she had imagined it. The little girl inside of her tried to somehow revive the boy she had been attracted to, to impose him on the shell of what he had become.

She was about to walk away when one last thing stopped her, and she glanced back at him. He was still watching her from her apartment door.

"Finley," she said. He looked puzzled, and so she clarified. "My name, it's Finley." And she left.

———

The morgue was as cold and dark as it was the last time she was here a couple of months ago when the father of one of the youngest and newest in their community had disappeared. Finley found him here, having been shot in the head point-blank. His chart said that he had been caught trying to steal an item of clothing from a shop in midtown, and the police had killed him on sight.

Finley remembered how it made her chest ache because it had been his daughter's birthday, and he was trying to steal a pink dress that the little girl had desperately wanted. It was cases like these that made her want to scream and wreck the entire city. She was so angry that one of her own had died, simply because he wanted to be able to give his daughter something special on her birthday.

From that day on, she swore to protect anyone else from ending up in here, lying lifeless and pale on the sterile metal carts, a blanket thrown carelessly over their still features. The morgue was rarely every staffed; there were so few medical personnel who had survived the journey to Garwick that they had to use their resources wisely.

The dead were dead, nothing more, and so it was only ever busy when some poor staff member came in to log and dispose of the bodies that had arrived over the course of a couple days. Luckily for Finley, today wasn't one of those days, and so unlocking one of the small above-ground windows wasn't just easy, but almost completely risk-free.

She stood in the darkness that had enveloped her, letting the chill air that came with being underground seep into her bones, and tried to calm the fire of her nerves. Instead, she flicked on her torch and began searching the tables for any sign of her friend. The figures lying there were creepy, their bodies mere shadows underneath the white cloth highlighted by her torchlight.

Moving over to the first table, she read the card that hung from the body's toe.

Caucasian, brunette, female, late 20s.

Finley held her breath; she couldn't smell the dead bodies. They were thoroughly cleaned, and the entire place was filled to the brim with disinfectant, but somehow, she could still imagine the scent of dead flesh crawling up her nose. It made her want to gag.

Steeling herself, she moved her hand forward and lifted the cloth, heaving a sigh of relief when the young woman on the table wasn't Jenny.

The relief was short-lived, however, as a sadness overtook her next. The young girl was pretty, her features small and delicate. Finley could imagine her face lit up with a smile or laughter, and she mourned for the life she never even had a chance to touch. She whispered the girl a silent prayer for peaceful rest, and then re-covered her body, preserving her dignity as much as she could.

Moving on, Finley checked the three other bodies that were lying on the carts, all of them either too old or too male. Already tired, she then moved over to the drawers on the far side of the wall, knowing that there could still be bodies she had to check. She hated the drawers as she would have to touch the bodies to read their labels, and the idea of touching the dead made her skin crawl. Not because they were dirty or anything, but a part of her had always worried that, somehow, death would manage to crawl its way into her and infect her with its darkness.

It was a childhood fear that she had never grown out of.

Finley was about to reach up and open the first drawer when a clanking sound made her flinch and freeze. Silently, she tried to listen for the sound of a guard, but all she could hear was the sound of her slightly panicked breaths. She stood there for a few minutes before she dug up the courage to open the drawer and check the tag. Old woman, not Jenny.

When she moved over to the next drawer, she started to read the tag when she swore she heard another sound and stopped once more.

This time when she stopped, however, she heard it again, the slight rattle of steel against steel. Senses on high alert, Finley tried to sense where the noise was coming from and was drawn toward the last drawer on the row. She left her current one, door open, and crept up to the final space. As she walked closer, that small sound grew louder and louder until it made her shake every time she heard it, as if at any second, a body would crawl out from its hole and try to eat her like an Antiqua.

Her hand was resting on the door when it stopped all of a sudden, and silence rained upon her. It was almost worse than the sound. The door opened with a quiet *whoosh*, and the body seemed to carry the vague scent of flesh—this time, not a figment of her overactive imagination.

Tentatively, she reached her hand forward for the tag, the browned paper hanging off the big right toe. Her fingers were on the course paper when the leg seemed to jolt, shocking her as if it were a snake striking at her, and she screamed when arms closed around her shoulders.

In a blind panic, she flailed, fighting to loosen the grip of whatever held onto her, only stopping when she heard a familiar grunt as her elbow caught her assailant's gut. Spinning out of their loosened grip, she screamed, "Kingsley?! What the hell are you doing here?"

He straightened himself, but she could still see the redness of his cheeks in the dark. "Your friend isn't here," he simply said.

"How do you know?"

He looked at her, and she could see the truth in his eyes. She didn't know why she trusted him. She didn't want to, and he had done nothing to warrant her trust. But still, she found herself stepping away, closing the drawer, and climbing back out into the moist air of the city.

It almost seemed too bright now with the sun beating down on her, but she was grateful to not be surrounded by shadows. She watched with apprehension as Kingsley followed her out through a passageway that looked too small for him, with the gracefulness of a slender cat.

When Finley realized that she had been staring at him for far too long, she turned on her heel, frustrated with herself and what she hadn't discovered in the morgue, but Kingsley's quiet voice interrupted her.

"You should drop this; it's for your own good."

It wasn't until Finley saw the devastation from the fight the previous night that she realized the scale of what was going on. The dining hall was in absolute chaos, with broken wood and splinters scattered across the floor, along with bloody cutlery and the bodies of a dozen different people.

Some she knew; some were unfamiliar, even to her.

The place had been swarming with cops when she went back the next day, and she thought she'd have to hang around and wait until nightfall to search the scene for any clues, but one glance at her now permanently scowling shadow, and they let her through with rushed apologies.

Sometimes, it paid to be stalked by her own little mercenary.

Looking through the mess, she sighed in frustration and kicked a piece of glass that tinkled its way across the debris.

"What?" Kingsley asked in a deadened tone, with no interest to back up his question.

Seeing no point in keeping her investigation from him, she said, "It's just… None of this makes sense. There's no catalyst to the fight, no obvious place where it started. One second, everyone was fine, and the next—"

"Boom," he jumped in, and she glanced at him in surprise but nodded.

"Yeah, boom."

He tilted his head with understanding but offered her no more information, which continued to bother here. It was the most frustrating thing, having all the answers right next to her but trapped inside an uptight ninja man with a frown practically ironed onto his ass.

Determined to get answers, despite the radio silence from the macho man next to her, she left the scene in search for some of the people who had been amongst the crowd last night. In comparison to how many Finley had seen fighting, she knew there must've been a few survivors, and she'd seen people flee during the event as well.

Any one of them might've seen something that was helpful. But the problem with finding people who had no home was that she never quite knew where they would be. Which commenced a day of playing cat and mouse in search for witnesses. By mid-day, she had caught up with a grand total of three, none of whom had stuck around long enough to have seen anything useful.

Walking away from the last witness, an elderly woman named Susan who had helped teach Finley how to read, Finley felt as if she were ready to scream. Even with Susan's kind and encouraging words, she just felt like she was missing something that was right in front of her.

The next person she ran into, Finley knew hadn't been at the shelter last night. Sammy was one of the few homeless citizens who had a job that paid well enough so that he could afford food—if not shelter. What stopped her, though, was the look on his face.

Usually, the kid was confident and arrogant, hiding the fear that came with being homeless with a tough guy disguise, but today he looked worried, which spooked her more than anything she had seen over the past day or so.

"Hey, Sammy, you feeling okay?" she called, and his eyes flickered to hers as if she had just startled him. It took a moment, but he managed to plaster a coy smile on his face.

"Yeah, Hood, all good," he deflected.

"You sure? You don't look so good. There's something strange happening lately, and I just want to make sure you're okay. You know you can always talk to me, right?" Her words seemed to hit him because he suddenly dropped his smile and rubbed at his throat, a look of concern more suited for someone twice his age.

"Well, the thing is, that... Nah, no, it's fine. I shouldn't—"

"Sammy, you can tell me," she encouraged him.

He rubbed the back of his head. "Some of my boys have gone missing. I thought it was a joke at first, but I can't find them anywhere," he confessed.

"For how long?" she asked.

"A week," he mumbled, scuffing his boots on the concrete.

"A week?! Sammy, why didn't you come get me sooner?!"

"I-I don't know. I thought—" He looked truly complexed by it all, and her caring nature kicked in enough that she lowered her voice and pulled the kid in for a brief hug.

"It's okay, Sammy. I get it. People come and go around here all the time," Finley whispered, making pointed eye contact with Kingsley, who was watching the exchange with a guarded look. "Can you tell me anything about how they were acting before they disappeared? Were they behaving oddly? Maybe they'd gone to get the vaccine at some point?"

Sammy shook his head. "Nah, they were fine the last time I saw them, and we were avoiding the vaccine, just like you told us to."

Finley nodded, but inside, she was staggering. If they hadn't been acting strange, and they hadn't taken the vaccine, then maybe this was all a lot more complicated than she had ever imagined.

"Is it my fault, Fin? Did I not look after them right?"

Sammy asked her, his eyes vulnerable in a way she hadn't seen since he was a little boy with boogers constantly hanging from his nose. The boys that followed him were younger by a few years, all having lost any parents they had, and Sammy took pride in inviting them into his own little gang of lost boys. They might look intimidating on the outside, but everyone in the community knew that they were mostly harmless, just some scared kids trying to find their place in the world.

"Nah, Sammy, none of this is your fault. Jenny is missing, too." Finley's voice trailed off, regretting having just given up that piece of information, but also knowing that it would comfort the boy.

"Really?!" Sammy exclaimed. "Her, too?"

Finley frowned. *Her, too.* Did that mean others had gone missing apart from the boys and her friend?

"Sammy, has anyone else gone missing lately?" she asked him. He looked puzzled.

"Well, yeah, a whole bunch. I thought you were already looking for them."

She nodded her head distractedly, looking around as if a line of people would appear with their list of missing names. "I am now. Can you tell me who else?"

"I don't remember who, but I know that old Mag said she was going to talk to you about it."

Old Mag was a woman who had practically raised Finley, and someone she hadn't heard from in months. It wasn't unusual that they'd go long periods without talking. Old Mag was the pillar of the community, a trusted confidant to all, but Finley liked to imagine that she could rely on her to get in touch when she needed her. Or at least, she had until now.

Scuffing up the boy's hair, Finley gave him a reassuring goodbye, sending him on his way and looking at Kingsley's accusatorily.

"Did you know about this?" she asked.

"Know about what?" he replied, and she stomped her boot on the ground. It was petulant, and his unreactive mask irritated her even more.

"Never mind," she muttered, turning and walking away, pulling a notepad out of her jacket pocket along with a pencil. Ignoring Kingsley's inquisitive looks, she began to jot down the names of the boys who had gone missing, the ones that Sammy had listed for her.

———

She spent the rest of the afternoon stopping anyone she came across and asking them if they knew someone or of someone who had gone missing, and by the end of the day, her list was five pages long. It baffled her how so many people could vanish, and not only had she not been told about it, but no one had mentioned it either.

Finley wanted to stop and beat herself up for not noticing it sooner, but she knew it would help no one. She stopped in her tracks when a large body slammed against her shoulder as she walked past, and already in a bad mood, Finley grabbed onto his arm.

"Hey! Big guy, I'm walking here," she barked, but he didn't turn to her, his large form simply swaying in her grasp. It was then that a sick feeling started to crawl up her throat.

"Hey…" But then Kingsley grabbed her shoulder. "Ouch, stop it!" She tried to shake him off, but he was persistent.

"We need to go," he mumbled, but he refused to look at her or the man she was still holding. Realizing that she wouldn't be able to break free from his grasp, she turned to the man she was holding, the queasy feeling intensifying when he twisted easily.

She gasped when she met his vacant gaze, his eyes open and bloodshot, and his mouth half-open. Flies were perched on his eyeballs, and blood was trickling from his nose and ears. She let him go as quickly as possible, backing up and knocking into Kingsley. The sight was grotesque and completely unexplainable to her.

It was obvious that the big man had been in a fight. The one last night or not, she couldn't tell for sure, but his nose was crooked from a recent break, and his wounds were only hours old. She waved her hand in front of his face, the flies spooking and passing away in a hurricane of little black bodies that made her want to vomit, but the man remained still. His chest was rising and falling slowly, but little else.

"What the hell?" Finley whispered, and she looked over at Kingsley. "What is this?" she asked, but before she could say anything else, a little girl tugged at the fabric that surrounded her legs.

When she looked down, she recognized her as Grace, daughter to Mary and George. She quickly moved her away from the formless man, trying to hide the gruesome sight of his face.

"What is it, honey?" she asked.

"It's mommy! Please, she's hurt," the little girl cried, her eyes red and puffy from what had to have been crying, and her small form was shaking.

Without asking a second time, Finley followed her little steps, not looking back to see if Kingsley followed her or not. A monster like him would probably laugh at the little girl's pain anyway.

What they found in the damp alley a few minutes away was enough to make Finley want to hurl up the contents of her stomach for the third time that night, but she gulped them down and tried to breathe through her mouth.

Grace's mother was pale, with sweat beading on her face, her breaths shallow and panting. Her hands were cupping her stomach, which was a mass of red, and on closer inspection, she could see that she was cradling her intestines in an effort to stop them from spilling out.

Finley quickly pulled Grace away.

"Sweetie, I need you to stay here while I try to help your mom. Can you tell me what happened?"

The little girl began to cry again, but managed to stutter, "W-we were at din-diner last night wh-when this f-fight broke out."

Finley hushed her when her tears began to fall heavier, and her words became garbled. "It's okay, Grace. I'm going to help your mommy, okay?"

"You already are," Grace mumbled and pointed behind her.

Finley glanced over at the woman who was still hunched over and dripping blood, and she gasped when she saw Kingsley kneeling in front of her. Scared for the woman's life, she ran over, grabbing at his shoulder.

"Hey! What do you think you're doing?"

But when she looked at him, Finley could see that he had been trying to pack the woman's bloody organs back inside her body.

"I'm helping her."

CHAPTER
NINE

Finley didn't get a chance to talk to Kingsley until later that evening, walking away from the hospital that they had managed to get Mary and her daughter to. The doctors informed them that it would be very unlikely, but they'd try their best to save Mary. Nothing was guaranteed, even with such advanced medical technology, but there was no use in standing around for news that Finley had no influence over when she could be out helping others.

Tired and with her nerves frayed, Finley pulled out

the notepad and looked at all the names she had written down. She knew over half of them, on either a name-only basis or have been friends with in some way. Hell, she'd celebrated birthdays with some of these people, played with their children when she was younger, known them since she had woken up on this godforsaken planet. Fighting back tears, she added one more name to the list.

Jenny.

Had she known about all the missing people? Had she gone looking for them? And why wouldn't she have told Finley about it? She could have helped!

Trying to distract herself from the self-doubt creeping in, she turned to Kingsley who, for once, looked drawn out and drained.

If she didn't know any better, she would've said that he was worried for Mary and Grace.

"Hey," she probed, her tone carrying less hostility than she had intended for it to, "what was that back there?"

But Kingsley shook his head and ran his hands through his disheveled black curls like he'd been doing for the past hour—obviously a nervous tick he had brought with him from his childhood, as she remembered him doing the same thing when they were younger. It was one of her few memories. Feeling caught off by the tenderness the memory brought her toward the man in front of her, she pushed him, even though she knew he was likely standing on a cliff's edge with his own emotions.

"Come on, ninja boy. What's wrong? She didn't die

like you wanted her to? We could always go back and pull the plug—"

"Stop it!" he yelled, the anger in his tone so foreign to her that she jumped. "For fuck's sake, Fin! Did you not see her? She'd been gutted! Probably because you can't keep your goddamn hands out of this!"

Her heart fell at the insinuation that she had somehow been the reason why this had happened, the guilt piling itself onto the self-doubt she had been cultivating for herself. "Hang on a second! How is this my fault? You're the murderer here! You've probably killed hundreds of my people! For what? Those stupid men and women who watch us from their towers like we're rats on a wheel?!"

"Yes!" he snapped. "I murder and mutilate in the name of those men and women. And I smile as I watch their blood drain from their neck."

She was taken aback by his words. She knew that he wasn't the boy she had once loved, but she couldn't imagine that he had turned so bad. He was indifferent, but she thought it was because he didn't care, not because... no.

"I don't believe you," she whispered, but her own voice was hoarse.

Kingsley grabbed onto that thread and pulled, a sick smile spreading across his face. "Yes, Fin. I love killing. I love it because, one day, it will bring an end to this entire despicable city!"

"There are innocent people here, Kingsley! People who deserve to live!"

"No one deserves to live! Humans are a plague that needs to be wiped away!" he yelled, and Finley could hear the desperation in his voice. But somehow, she just couldn't believe that he truly wished harm upon the people of Roseallan City. She had watched him save that woman and child from his superiors, and even patch up Mary so they could drag her to the hospital. Hell, he had saved her life yesterday. This wasn't a man who didn't care.

"Kingsley…," she whispered to him, her voice quiet. But she was distracted from what she was about to say when the sound of a fight broke out just a few yards away.

Without pausing, she started running, following the sound of rabid howls and the thud of flesh against flesh. Kingsley called after her, but she didn't stop.

And what she ran into made absolutely no sense. In front of her, John, sweet, sweet John, was locked in combat with a younger homeless woman that Finley didn't recognize. On the ground, two cups of what she assumed was his wine laid scattered, and the two were fighting mindlessly. Without thinking, Finley jumped into the fray.

"John!" she screamed when he grabbed onto the woman's hair and pulled a chunk out. She tried to pull his arms away, but he was stronger than he looked. "John, what's going on?! We need to talk about this!" But John didn't seem to hear her or see her. He kept making these savage half screams, the same sounds as the woman he was fighting. Neither of them turned their attention to her, and the bruises and cuts were beginning to build. John's lip was swollen and bloody; the woman's right eye was black and blue.

She then felt Kingsley's arm on her shoulder, trying

to pull her away, but she shook him off. "No," she screamed, "I have to save them!" and then she lunged back into the fray.

———

Kingsley's heart nearly jumped out of his chest as he watched Finley run back into the fight. His instincts screamed at him to stop her, to protect her from the truth. That she couldn't save these people… or any of her people. They were all doomed, just like he was.

He hadn't meant what he said earlier, not entirely, anyway. He didn't enjoy killing or watching these people die. But knowing what he did? He couldn't help but feel that a quick death would be a gift. With what his people had planned for hers, it was too horrifying to even think about.

When one of the woman's outstretched hands hit Finley in the face, leaving a bloody scratch down her cheek, he couldn't stop himself from rushing forward to try and help her. He knew it would be in vain. No one would be able to stop these two, but he could try and help Finley feel a little less powerless.

He didn't know why he cared so much about how she felt. They had known each other a grand total of a day and a half, but he felt drawn to her inexplicably. At first, it had just been because she reminded him of the girl he'd lost when he was just a child; being near her had soothed a part of his soul he thought was completely ruined.

But after watching her, seeing how the people of this community relied on her, and how much she cared for them in return, he couldn't help but be enthralled by her determination. She was a spark of light in a world that seemed endlessly dark, and even though he knew it was selfish, he couldn't help but want to stay and bask in her light for a little longer. To pretend, for just a moment, that he was also one of the people she cared about.

It was funny, really, the cold assassin seeking affection from the rabid vigilante. But he had stopped questioning these things ever since his life had been turned upside down back when Earth was destroyed.

Part of him wanted to destroy her. She was a weakness, a vulnerability, something someone could use against him. It was as if he had taken out his very heart and let it walk around unprotected. He hated the feeling of vulnerability. But at the same time, he felt drunk on her company, on how she made him feel.

Focusing back on the fight, he pulled at the man while Finley tried to focus on the woman, dragging them apart. But even when they had been separated, they savagely reached for each other, trying to tear each other apart.

"John!" Finley pleaded, her voice raw and distraught. "Please, stop!"

But the man didn't hear her, and they grew more and more unsettled the longer they were held apart. When the woman wouldn't give up, Finley yelled and reached for the blade at her thigh. In one quick movement, she slit the woman's throat, and the woman dropped to the ground lifeless, her blood spilling from her throat.

The change in the man, John, was instant. No longer

trying to kill the woman, he turned his attention to Kingsley and Finley, his arms grabbing for her.

Before she could scream, Kingsley grabbed his head and twisted it, hearing the familiar crack of his vertebrate breaking. Finley sobbed as the man's limp body fell to the ground. He wanted to help her, to hold onto her, and stop the tears that were running from her eyes.

In this light, the brave and indestructible girl he had come to know was gone, and in its place, was a young woman who was frightened. It made him angrier than he had ever felt, and for the first time, his mind rebelled at the idea that this whole situation was immovable.

Surely, there was *something* he could do. To save her, to save her people.

He was about to reach forward to touch her shaking shoulders when something from above caught his eye.

A figure crouched low against the darkness of the roofs above, watching them below. When it realized that Kingsley had seen it, it sprinted off, its movements too smooth and practiced to be anything other than a mercenary. They were trained in spying and reconnaissance.

Without a word, he followed in pursuit, He could hear Finley beside him, and he felt a burst of pride as she kept up. She had seen the figure as well and come to the same conclusion—they couldn't leave it alive.

The unknown made Kingsley stomach churn. It couldn't have been Strage; the figure was too small, and he wouldn't do something as menial as spying on Kingsley. But it could've easily been Ivan or some other little minion. And if they reported to Strage what he had done? Killing the test subjects on the streets with the help of a young woman? Not only would his life be at risk, but so would Finley's. And no way was he going to let that happen.

Kingsley sprinted as hard as he could, twisting and turning down alleyways, keeping the figure in his line of sight. He would've chased it forever if Finley hadn't suddenly pulled him to a stop. It wasn't until he looked down that he realized he was about to run into the widest part of the canal, the water there quick and deep enough to drown him, that he realized the figure had been leading him into the trap.

He stomped his foot and looked down at Finley, who looked up at him with concern. Someone had seen them put down two people, and now they had gotten away, the figure long vanishing into the night. It wouldn't be long before someone came knocking on their door, and they both knew that they wouldn't be coming to pat them on the back.

"What do we do?" Finley asked, her voice faint. And for the first time, Kingsley had no idea.

He just shook his head and said, "Pray."

CHAPTER
TEN

Finley held her breath as she watched Kingsley pace back and forth. He was openly agitated, and that alone told her how dire the situation was. She didn't have to be a genius to know that someone watching them from above and then running off wasn't a good sign.

Her eyes were still stiff from crying after having to kill John and the woman, but she didn't blame Kingsley. He tried to hold John back so that she could get in between the two of them, but nothing seemed to reach them. It was almost like they weren't even there anymore, like two savage Antiqua.

Her heart dropped at the realization that their behavior was so similar to the beasts that roamed outside of the wall. But surely, she would know if she'd been fighting one of them, right? And they would've been killing the other citizens all day, not just at night.

No. Not Antiqua, but something very much like it.

She gulped and focused on Kingsley's still tense form to try and calm herself. When she stepped up to him, she could hear him muttering about mistakes and something happening again. None of it made sense, and when she reached her hand out to his arm, he flinched away as if she had just burnt him.

"Hey, Kingsley, what's wrong? What are we going to do?" she asked, trying to keep her tone even and not expose the panic in her head.

Kingsley snorted, and Finley was caught off guard by the dismissive sound. "There is no we."

"Kingsley, I know we said some things, but—"

"No!" he shouted. "There is no we, and there's not going to be a we! I've been following you for far too long, trying to get you to stop this wild chase of yours, when really, I should just let you get yourself killed."

Taken aback, Finley dropped her hand, taking a few steps away. "Kingsley? Is that why you've been following me?" she asked, not quite sure of what he was saying.

His cackling laughter made her heart drop. "You thought I was following you around because I like you?" he taunted. "I'm sorry, but I'm not attracted to dirty, little street rats," he spat.

Without even thinking, her hand was moving, and a satisfying slap filled the humid night air. Kingsley went silent for a moment before laughing again, but Finley refused to stick around to hear him insult her any longer. Turning around, she ran, leaving him behind in the darkness.

She was angry at him. Sure, his words had been hurtful, but most of all, she was angry at herself. She was an independent person. She didn't rely on anyone else to validate her or make her feel safe, and yet, she had somehow become attached to Kingsley to the point where he was capable of hurting her.

She was usually good at predicting the worst. Living on the streets for so long had knocked any optimism out of her, and she felt safe whenever she was either right or pleasantly surprised. She didn't like being caught off guard; she preferred being prepared for any situation that came along, and she never expected the best of anything to happen.

It rarely ever did.

But somehow, she had hope in Kingsley, probably putting her faith in that old image she had of him, that slightly older boy who held her when she was sad and put bandages on her cuts. She couldn't help but see him as a protector, and she instinctively leaned toward him to help her.

Well, he'd shown her just how wrong she was.

And Finley never made the same mistake twice.

Trying to banish her emotions from her mind, she stopped in an empty alley, panting, the ache in her chest distracting her from the void that Kingsley's absence seemed to have left. These streets were her home, but for some reason, she felt vulnerable without him.

She shook her head.

There was one person she still had to see, someone who had been aware of all this and hadn't told Finley—Old Mag. It was time to drop by for a little visit.

Old Mag wasn't just the leader of their small community. There was an otherworldly presence to her that made her feel mystical. Whenever Finley found herself near her, it just seemed as if Old Mag knew more about Finley than Finley ever knew about herself.

Others said she was a prophet, an oracle. And while Finley had a hard time seeing her as anything other than her proxy mother, she could see where the rumors came from. And right now, she was betting on them being true.

The path to the old woman's shack was long and winding. She holed up in the same place she always had. It was the closest thing there was to a proper house around here, a warehouse on the outskirts of the city. She lived in the office above, her small rooms cluttered and homely, and below, she provided shelter for those who needed somewhere warm and dry to sleep. There wasn't enough room for everyone, of course. Just the weakest of the weak and children who couldn't defend themselves.

It was hidden away deep within the district. Old Mag had chosen the furthest place possible from the homes of the rich. And as a byproduct, none of the authorities could ever find it in the maze of the Hopeless District, and no one in the community would ever give it up.

It had been a lesson from Old Mag that Finley learned to keep her home a secret. That was until Kingsley barged in…

Opening the side door to the warehouse, Finley moved quietly, trying not to disturb the many sleeping bodies inside. They were of all shapes and sizes, some missing limbs and some petite, but all of them were in very poor conditions, and Finley's heart ached for them. She crept up the stairs to the office, where a dim light indicated that Mag was still awake. The old bag never seemed to sleep.

She let herself in quietly, listening for the sound of the old woman. When she heard nothing but the crackle of fire, she called out softly, "Mag?"

"What the hell you doin' here at this hour?" Mag asked from close beside her, making Finley jump from the shock.

But Finley laughed when she saw the old woman's wicked smile; Mag had always been a prankster. "Hello to you, too, Old Mag."

"Don't be calling me 'old' now," she tutted, waddling back over to her seat beside the fire, her favorite shawl laying there next to her. Mag was a pale woman in her late 60s and still very active for her age. She was big and soft, both in her body and mind, but she was also sharp as a pin and the wisest person Finley had ever met.

"Sit down, sit down," Mag fussed, and Finley smiled when a steaming mug of hot tea was placed in front of her.

"Knew I was coming, eh?" she teased, and Mag snorted.

"I always know when you're coming. The whispers reach me far before you ever do."

"And what have those whispers been telling you about the disappearances?" Finley asked, getting straight to the point.

She didn't like the way Mag's face fell at the words. "Ah, so you've heard about those."

"Yeah, I have, and I was surprised to hear that you found out about them a while ago and failed to mention it," Finley pressed, trying not to be rude but hurt that Mag had kept something so important from her.

"Well, I haven't seen you in a while—"

"Cut the crap, Mag. We both know you could've gotten to me if you wanted to." Finley observed the woman she had known for nearly her entire life, the woman she had come to see as a mother. But now, she just looked like a fragile old woman. Her face was drawn, and her eyes crinkled in a way that mapped out years of stress. Sympathy overtook her impatience, and Finley soon calmed down. "Come on, Mag. What's going on here?"

The woman sighed and looked up at her. "I've been keeping this from you, but not for the reason you think." She paused and looked into the fire. "Let me explain. There was a boy, a long time ago, who was lost—"

"Mag, can we skip the story?" Finley asked impatiently but silenced herself when Mag shot her a look.

"Do you want me to tell you or not?" Finley nodded her head, and Mag continued. "As I was saying, there was a boy, and he was lost. Not in body. He knew where he was physically, but in his soul. His mother had long departed the world, her warm impression fading slowly over time under the cold hand of his father. He was a good boy, with a good heart, but even a flower that grows in the dark has to twist to suit its environment. And so, this young boy, he changed, changed until not even the one he loved most could recognize him. And that person, the girl he loved, she had the power to help him, to change everything. She was unique and special, but the price of his soul? It would be both of their lives. Now this young boy and girl, they thought they could do it; they were in love and felt hope for the future, but they were also young and naïve, and their hopes were the death of them." Mag held her hand out, and Finley instinctively grabbed it, not watching as the old woman brought a blade to her wrist.

"What does this have to do with the disappearances, Mag?" she asked, frustrated and trying to ignore the chill that skittered up her spine, along with a feeling of doom.

But before the woman could say anything, a shadow moved across the window nearby, so quickly that Finley didn't know what was happening before Kingsley suddenly appeared, crouched over her body protectively, holding the knife that had been at her wrist up to Mag's wrinkling neck.

His face was cold enough to freeze blood, with aggression pouring from him. But Mag didn't look scared; she only smiled knowingly and said, "About time, boy. I was beginning to think you wouldn't come." She croaked. And he looked just as baffled as Finley did.

CHAPTER
ELEVEN

K ingsley was beating himself up. But this wasn't necessarily strange or new. He'd spent most of his life punishing himself for stupid mistakes he'd made when he was younger that he could never take back. However, he was so used to agonizing over the past, and now that he was stuck on something in the present, he couldn't help but feel… different.

He was used to the feeling of uselessness. His past mistakes were so far gone that there was nothing he could do to touch them. They were written in stone, unchangeable and immobile. He prayed at the altar of his own tribulations and spilt his blood daily for the gods who haunted his every waking moment with memories. Now… now the issue was here, in front of him. And while he told himself that he would leave her, he could do nothing but obsess.

She was there in the city this very moment. He could touch her, apologize, talk to her, and bear his soul. The part of him that hated himself told him to stop, to just walk away, to do as he had said and leave. But the part of him that still housed his younger self, the one who was frozen inside his turmoil, wanted to run to her and beg for forgiveness. It made him feel both weak and powerful at the same time.

He had this creature, this beautiful and fiery creature now in his life, and he wanted to have her permission to stay with her, to watch her as she burned like a beacon in this never-ending night.

And so, it was that desire that pulled him to follow her. He knew Finley didn't want to see him. After all, the things he had said were hurtful. That was his purpose, after all, his never-failing mechanism to keep himself isolated. He always seemed to know exactly what to say to people to hurt them. Maybe because he knew which barbs dug the deepest in himself.

Kingsley crept along the roofs of the buildings, following Finley deep into the Hopeless District. The protective part of himself wanted to be there at her side, glued to her so that nothing could cause her harm. But he had to remember that the streets she walked were the streets of her home, and while they looked like a veritable animal trap to him, to her, they were the familiar streets of her childhood. It made him sad knowing that while he and his detestable brethren had been living in the sterile finery of the inner sanctum, vulnerable girls and boys like Finley had been trying to survive on these harsh streets.

He knew the homeless and poor here banded together, formed a small community that was interconnected enough where the state felt it was necessary to monitor, but no amount of friendly faces and warm smiles could put food in bellies or stop the rain from soaking old rags on a winter's night. Truly, he was baffled that the homeless community continued to grow, not just amongst those who fell from money, but amongst the children born into it.

It was so easy to think of them as static, barely human elements of the city herself. But somewhere, there must be men and women who fell in love, who started families together in this harsh environment. How was it that these people not only survived, but flourished in their impoverished environment in a way that even the rich could not?

Perhaps money was the factor. Perhaps his people had been so hardened by their want for power that they were no longer capable of flourishment. Only destruction.

Following Finley's tracks got harder and harder as she moved deeper and deeper into the maze of desolate buildings. At times, Kingsley even lost her, her small physique fading into the shadows as if she never were. During those times, he felt his heart rate speed up, thudding against the wall of his ribs like some sort of jackhammer. He would rush from roof to roof, searching for any glimpse of her, until finally, he would catch a glint of her leather jacket under the moonlight.

Wherever she was going required secrecy, as she retraced her steps several times and went in circles. If anyone else had been trailing her, someone less obsessed with her, they would've lost her by now. But not him. He would stay on her toe, whether she knew it or not.

It wasn't until much later that Finley stopped, looked up at a building with a warmth that seemed out of place in this district. The building she stared at was a large warehouse that had probably once been for storage. The roof had collapsed from the taller building next to it until the warehouse underneath was barely visible.

The perfect hiding place, really.

The back of his neck prickled with awareness, and Kingsley quickly surveyed his surroundings. He could see a dim light coming from the window of the far side, likely where the overseer's office would've been. He thought he caught the shifting of shadows slipping through the dark, but it was gone so swiftly that he thought he must have imagined it.

When he looked back down to where he last saw Finley, she was no longer there. Frustrated and more than a little panicked, he leapt onto the collapsing roof, freezing when the whole thing groaned precariously. He remained still until he felt the old brick and timber beneath him settle once more, making a note to move much more lightly. Pushing his black curls from his face, Kingsley moved quietly over the broken and splintered wood that had long been grown over with moss and ivy, looking for any entrance into the building below… if there even was one.

He released a sigh when he finally found the smallest gap into the cavern below. The first thing he saw were beds, at least fifty of them, lined in orderly rows on the floor of the warehouse. The space, contrary to what it might look like on the outside, was dry and clean, with hay on the inside to try and make the space feel less desolate.

Kingsley watched a bit longer and soon realized that below him, slept the children of the district, their small bodies rising and falling in slumber. It occurred to him that what he had just found wasn't a secret meeting place of the poor, but their nursery. The place they had to protect at all costs, like a wolf pack protected the cave of their young.

His chest tightened with the weight of the knowledge he was now privy to. What he had stumbled upon was what the state had been looking for years for. The poor were a law unto themselves, their number far outgrowing that of the rich. And while they were kept in an illusion of powerlessness because of the money they didn't have, the rich knew they had to tread carefully around them. They had been looking for a long time to find where their weakness was, the children who increased their ranks every year. So far, it had remained a mystery, safe from the clutches and harms of his mercenary brothers and sisters.

Now… Now he had this information. The mercenary in himself, for there was one—one as ruthless as his kin—knew he should share this with his people. He would be celebrated, congratulated, and it would certainly annoy Strage.

But truth was, he didn't want to tell them.

He had no love for his people; they were murderous and bloodthirsty. Their loyalty wasn't to him, and so why should his loyalty be to them? And loyalty wasn't a word they were familiar with, only blackmail and leverage. And this lovely flame he had stumbled across, the one who had defended him even when she didn't know him, maybe that was what loyalty was. Her presence had touched him and sparked something within him that he hadn't felt in years.

Hope.

When he looked at Finley, he felt hope. For her, for her city and her people, and maybe even for himself. If she could grow up the way she had and still be the woman she was today, perhaps there was a chance for humanity.

When Finley crept up the stairs toward the office room, he adjusted his position, returning to the adjacent building so he could peer in through the window. The glass was murky and fogged, the warmth within creating condensation on the glass, but he could see enough to see a slender figure meet a shorter, rounder one.

When he moved closer, he saw that she was talking with an older woman, the type of older woman with graying hair that resembled home and protection.

Kingsley never had a grandmother or maternal figure in his life, not for the longest time, but he liked to imagine that if he had, she would be something like this woman.

Finley interacted with her with familiarity, giving her smiles and smirks that Kingsley had seen only briefly himself. A part of him was desperate to see her look at him in the same way, like he meant something to her.

They embraced each other, and then moved to the fire that burned at the end of the room, taking their places opposite one another as if it were some sort of ritual. It had him wondering what their exact relationship was.

He'd heard the rumors. It was his job to know and hear every tale that crossed the mouths of the citizens of Roseallan City. A story about a woman who could read the future, who would protect them and guide them to safety. He used to think it was just a myth, sprouted by desperate minds looking for some sort of hope in their desolate existences. But now, looking at this picture, instincts that had long died out in his human body sparked to life, speaking to him in a language he didn't understand.

Be careful, they warned. *Tread carefully. You are in the presence of that which is unknown.*

And because of this, he didn't hesitate when the flash of a blade caught in the firelight, his body coiling like a viper as he sprung forward, knocking the window open and rolling in front of Finley protectively. The blade the woman had pulled was gripped in her hand, which was now engulfed by his larger one. He knew he should loosen it. The woman felt like paper, delicate enough to break, but his desire to keep Finley from harm was much larger and much fiercer.

When the woman began laughing, however, his

brain stalled, unable to connect the threat with the smiling face in front of him.

"About time, boy. I was beginning to think you wouldn't come," she croaked.

Startled, he dropped her hand and stepped back, kneeling beside Finley. He could feel her gaze on his face, feel her accusatory stare that he longed to meet, but he couldn't bring himself to take his eyes off the most unpredictable element in the room.

"Kingsley, what are you doing?!" came Finley's distraught voice, and while he knew she was angry, a part of him was released from tension.

She was speaking to him, even after the things he had said. She wasn't locked away from him completely, and he could rectify it still. When he didn't reply, Finley growled, an adorable sound that made him want to press his ear up against her chest and hear it from the source, feel it vibrate through his skin, but before she could say anything else, the woman spoke again.

"You think I'm a threat to the girl, Kingsley?" the woman interrogated, her slightly milky gaze meeting his own. A feeling of being seen pounded through him, the likes of which he had never felt, and he felt his limbs softening against his will until he was sat next to Finley like some sort of schoolboy. "Yes," she continued, "I know who you are, and I know what you were doing, spying on me and my girl." She smiled like she knew a secret everyone else was dying to know, but there was a sharpness to it that put Kingsley on edge.

"What are you talking about, Mag?" Finley asked, her tone light as if she hadn't felt threatened by the knife to her skin. Her voice relaxed him.

"Didn't you know? This boy here has been following you around like some lovesick puppy," Mag cooed. "You're losing your touch, my dear."

Finley sniffed indignantly. "Am not. I knew he was there."

Kingsley glanced over at her, but she avoided his gaze.

Mag laughed. "Of course, you did."

The comfortable back and forth between the two women put a dampener on Kingsley's battle instinct. Mag glanced at him, and it was as if a blanket was lifted from his shoulders before he even knew it was there. The woman was curious, but she definitely didn't pose any harm to him or Finley.

"Now," the woman said, her voice rough and lyrical at the same time, "you two have an appointment somewhere that you cannot be late for. Give me your hands."

Finley did so without hesitation, and guided by her ease, Kingsley reluctantly gave his own. He could've sworn that she chuckled at him as he did so, and his face turned red with embarrassment. However, that quickly dissipated when the old woman leaned forward and cut them both with the knife, the blood pooling into the bowl of water beneath them.

CHAPTER
TWELVE

Finley twitched slightly as she felt the familiar burn of a blade across her palm. The cut was small and superficial, but her awareness of it always made the pain feel that much sharper. She might've even gasped slightly if Kingsley wasn't right next to her after he kicked his way into the room.

She was still confused as to what he was doing there and how he'd managed to follow her when she was one of the best at losing trackers through the maze. But Mag seemed undisturbed by his presence, and so she figured she was in no immediate danger. In fact, it had almost been worth it just to see the slight blush that colored his cheeks, temporarily revealing a small glimpse of the boy she had once known.

It was a strange feeling, sitting next to Kingsley like she did when they were kids, looking up to an elder for answers. If she closed her eyes, she might be able to take herself back in time completely, turn the warm press of his much larger body back into the gangly presence it had once been. It wasn't that she preferred his looks when he was younger. He was a veritable sex god now, tall, dark, and handsome, but now he felt so far away. He was distant and cold, so while he was stunning, it was more like the perfection of a statue. Something to be cherished but could never be truly touched.

The boy he had been was real, with acne and unruly hair that he didn't know what to do with. His voice kept breaking, and he fell over himself like he still hadn't realized that he was growing like a weed. His imperfections were cute, and they brought her closer to him. Next to that boy, her own shortcomings weren't weaknesses, but qualities that made her endearing.

Now, she was in this strange place where she felt both connected to him and cut off from him, doomed to never be able to show him who she really was. And why would she even want to? He made it abundantly clear that he wasn't attracted to her, that he found her upbringing and status disdainful. Why should she care about him?

Fueled by her own internal monologue, Finley pulled her hand away from its contact with Kingsley's more aggressively than she should have, causing him to glance at her, and Mag to smile in that irritating way whenever she told her things that Finley didn't want to know.

Curse the old woman's sight to Hell and back.

"Stop with that sour face," Mag ordered. "You'll give yourself wrinkles."

Kingsley huffed in something that might've been a laugh, and Finley shot him her best glare. At the eye contact, he cleared his throat, but she swore she could see a flicker of humor in his green eyes. She huffed to herself and stuck her nose in the air, trying her best to seem unaffected. The hag laughed and shook her head before turning her attention to the bowl before them.

She dipped her wrinkled fingers into the mingling liquid, stirring it and beginning a strange low chant. Finley had heard it a thousand times throughout her life, but she still couldn't understand the words. It was almost as if the second they were uttered, they ceased to be, in memory and in echo. It always gave her a trippy feeling that she didn't like.

Mag then froze mid-chant, her fingers stilling in the water and her breath halting. The voice that Finley continued to hear no longer sounded like Mag's, but something rough and torn, as if her throat was bleeding.

"I see nothing clearly," Mag said, her accent disappearing. "A building, white with jagged metal walls. And a symbol in red on the front, like a Chinese character in a circle... the number thirteen. Wait, I see... I see blood! Blood, terror, and people screaming. There is pain in this place, terrible pain, people trapped in agony. I-I..." In a jolt, Mag kicked the bowl away from her, her breath panting and her eyes wild with fear. "No," she screamed, "get away!"

Surprised, Finley jumped forward, trying to calm down Old Mag, but her body shook underneath her hands, and for the first time, Finley could really see her age, feel her frail bones and paper soft skin. Finley hushed at her softly, rubbing her back and rocking her until she regained her composure, but even then, the cheeky woman she knew was absent.

"You should go," Mag whispered to her.

"What? I'm not leaving you; I don't even know where—"

"He knows," Mag interrupted, and her hazy eyes moved to where Kingsley sat behind them.

Finley turned to look at him, and a lump formed in her throat when he nodded his head subtly. *He knows? How's that possible?*

"Stay safe and rest up," Finley gave in and said firmly, knowing fully well that there was no use in arguing with the old woman. She knew her mind, and when it was made up, it was impossible to budge.

A small spark of life returned to Old Mag's eyes, and she waved the girl away. "Go, child. I'll be fine."

Finley sighed doubtfully but got up and left anyway, saying nothing to Kingsley on the way out. In truth, she didn't know how to feel about the man next to her. He'd said some harsh things to her, horrible things even, and he obviously didn't share her values. He worked for the state, for God's sake! And yet, the little girl inside of her ached. She wanted to reach forward and embrace him, tell him that she still cared for him. That little girl inside of her still believed that her young friend was still inside of him, just waiting to feel safe enough to come out.

————

Out on the streets, she stopped, turning to face Kingsley. She didn't have anything to say to him, so she opted for silence, using one of his own tricks against him. He cracked a few seconds later, looking at the ground and shuffling his feet like some sort of teenager who had been caught trying to look through the window of the girl's locker room. Ha, perhaps she should use this trick more often; it was obviously very effective.

"Finley, I—" He struggled for his words. "What I said wasn't completely true… I mean, some might think that way, and I-I can see why—No, no, that sounds wrong. What I mean is that I don't feel that way about you, in that the words that I said didn't convey—ah!"

Watching him stumble, big strong Kingsley looking all shy and awkward, made Finley crack an uncharacteristic laugh. One that wasn't scornful or sarcastic, but a true little chuckle. When he opened his eyes, he found Finley staring at him, his eyes trained on her mouth and a hot look in his eyes. It made something in her stomach squirm, and it was her own turn to blush.

"Look, lover boy, do you know where this place is or not?" She tried to appear cold, but instead, she just sounded like she was teasing. However, she was too preoccupied by her burning cheeks to change her tone.

"Ah, yes, yes, I do. Come, follow me," he said, and he turned, but instead of walking down the alley as she had expected him to, he walked over to the wall of one of the buildings.

"I'm pretty sure Diagon Alley was an Earth thing," she said, and he looked at her quizzically. "Really? You haven't read the Harry Potter books from Earth? Everyone was into them!"

He shook his head, his expression lost. "I didn't have time for entertainment. I spent a lot of time training." He said it like it wasn't the saddest thing in the world.

Finley didn't have to make too big of a jump to guess why Kingsley had become the man he was. She knew the rich were far from warm and loving people, and being raised like that as a child? They were lucky if they made it out with their sense of morality in check!

But to hear him make a statement like that with such apathy? It stabbed at that part of her that wanted to protect those she loved, and as much as she hated to admit it, the young Kingsley was still on that list.

She was shaken from her thoughts when he began to lift himself up onto the wall.

"Seriously, Kingsley, what are you doing?" she asked.

He looked back down at her, miraculously still ascending with complete surety, even while he looked at her and spoke. "If we take the route by road, it will take us all night to cross the city." He hopped up onto a window ledge, already dizzyingly high. "If we travel across the buildings, we can cut that time in half, and I assume you'd like to get there before dawn?"

She huffed out a breath, staring at the wall. He was right. It *would* take all night to cross the city if they were to use the roads, but traveling along the roofs? Was it even possible? Assessing the wall, she tried to remember the movements she had watched him make up the seemingly unclimbable surface. He was taller than her, and so some of the movements he made wouldn't be possible for her smaller frame. But she didn't have to match him; she just didn't want to fall flat on her face.

She touched the first brick tentatively, digging her fingers into the crevice and tugging lightly to see if it would hold. When she didn't immediately slip off, she quickly pulled herself half a foot off the ground. From there, she looked up at the rest of the wall, Kingsley's body a bare smudge in the shadows at the top. She took a few more slow steps, unsure and hesitant, but slowly continued to make progress. By the time she was three-quarters of the way up, her fingers and ankles were aching, and sweat was beading down her back.

So close, only a small amount of space left. But as she reached up her hand to grab the next hold, her ankle—which was shaking with effort—gave in, and with the sickening feeling of falling, Finley watched almost in slow motion as her body fell backwards.

On instinct, Finley closed her eyes, bracing for what was surely going to be a brutal impact on both her body and her pride. But before she could even register it, her body landed on a soft, warm surface instead of the cold, hard ground.

She didn't need to look up to know that Kingsley had caught her, but she did so anyway, looking into his bright green eyes with surprise. His face was different in this light, not the same wall of stone that she was used to, but somehow more open. More vulnerable. She could see the way his lips quivered slightly and his throat bobbed.

If she weren't hanging several feet above the ground, she might have wondered if they were about to kiss, but the pain in her arm was too much to bear.

"Are you going to let me hang here all night?" she prompted, and he quickly began lifting her the rest of the way, his strength still slightly shocking even though she'd seen it in action a few times already. "Thanks," she muttered at the top, dusting herself off.

He nodded but said nothing more, starting a slow jog over the roofs, which were a lot easier to travel along than she had initially thought. The buildings were so closely packed that the jumps over the alleys were like hopping over puddles. She also noticed that Kingsley sped up when he realized that she was keeping his pace more than effortlessly.

There was something thrilling about it, running alongside the man she both knew and didn't, the cold wind brushing against her warm skin, and adrenaline pumping through her like a toasty buzz. She felt both brutally alive and also as if she were dreaming, the moment seeming too unreal to be something she could actually experience.

She didn't know what was in store for them, where their paths would go, but she did know that despite her determination to stay away from him, they were connected. And that meant her life was changing before her eyes, and she had no idea what or who she was going to be at the end of it.

When they made it to the inner sanctum wall, Finley

came to a stop, her breath heavy but not uncomfortable. Annoyingly, Kingsley looked like he'd barely broken a sweat.

When he began to walk toward the wall, she halted, staring at the obstacle she had never been able to jump. She'd always craved to see behind the wall, to break through and examine every nook and cranny. But it had always been that impenetrable thing, the blockade that would never break.

"What's wrong?" Kingsley's low voice broke her from her reverie.

"I, ah, I can't get across," she confessed, and his expression almost frustrated her. Of course, he wouldn't understand what it was like to be short and limited to where she could go. He never had to face the problems that she did. The world was his playground, and he could come and go as he pleased.

He walked up to her, his steps swift, and his tall physique towered over her once again. But this time, instead of it feeling intimidating, it felt almost... welcoming. She didn't feel scared of him anymore. His hand landed on her shoulder, and her body leaned into him instead of away, acting as if it had its own will.

Kingsley's body responded in time. Consciously or not, she couldn't tell, but they were closer than they should be for two strangers.

"Finley, it's okay. I can get you across. What I said—"

You don't—" She went to interrupt him, but he shook his head.

"No, let me finish. What I said wasn't just incorrect; it was wrong. You have more integrity than all the people behind this wall put together, and it is I who should be grateful that I even got the chance to meet you. What I said is unforgivable, but I'm sorry."

She looked into his eyes, her heart thudding in her chest. Why couldn't she just hate this man like she should? She hated that her feelings felt so uncertain, that she couldn't see the road ahead of them.

"I don't know how to trust you," she whispered. And he nodded, a sad look in his eyes that she so desperately wanted to wipe away.

"I know," he murmured, "but you don't have to. Just... stay with me, by my side, for now." She didn't think either of them really knew what he was asking for. But she figured that they had time to figure it out... and much more important things to focus on right now.

Shaking her head, she stepped away from him, but the tension between them had shifted, now more relaxed than awkward. A mutual understanding of complete misunderstanding had been made, and in that ignorance, there was a certain safety to each other's company.

"Come on," he said, "we're not far away."

The rest of the journey was quiet, but the pace was relaxed if not insistent. When she climbed over the wall, she expected lights and blaring sirens, maybe even a shot or two, but they crossed over in silence, and the night didn't shift the rest of the way.

As Kingsley had said, the building was only a five-minute jog from the wall, standing alone like some sort of abandoned box, unlit and vast in the light.

"What is it?" Finley asked as they paused in front of it, just outside the reach of several cameras. On closer look, she could see that it was heavily guarded. What looked like a simple sliding door had a biometric lock system, as well as several hidden surveillance cameras and what looked like small gaps where guns could be pointed and fired from within.

"I'm not sure," Kingsley responded, but there was an odd tilt to his voice, like he knew something more that he wasn't telling her. "It's never been somewhere I've had to go."

She didn't believe him, but the expression on his face seemed to be telling the truth. "Well, it's now or never," she replied back, and she began to walk toward the building. She wasn't surprised when Kingsley's arm shot out in front of her. "What?" she asked.

He looked at a loss for words. "It's just, maybe we shouldn't go inside," he said.

She rolled her eyes, her face turning into a more serious look. "Kingsley, I'm going inside, whether you join me or not. I'm not waiting around all night." And with that, she continued on. Kingsley remained still behind her for a moment before following lightly.

Walking around the building, avoiding the major entryways that were all guarded by complicated locks, Finley scanned the building for a window or opening. The building was already behind a heavily-armed wall, so there must be some sort of gap… somewhere.

She smiled when she spotted a small window cracked open around the back, just big enough for someone like her to crawl through. She surveyed for cameras quickly, and when she came up blank, she ran over, looking up at it. It was just above her reach.

She looked back at Kingsley, who watched both her

and the building warily as if something would jump out at any minute and attack them.

"Give me a lift?" she asked, and he nodded, but he still seemed hesitant.

She almost wanted to ask him what's wrong, but she figured that if he wanted to tell her, he would.

When he stepped up to her, she felt his body heat, and her own body shivered when he touched her.

Goddamn traitorous heart.

She tried to ignore the feeling of his firm muscles as he lifted her onto his shoulders. She almost blushed again when her knees rested on them, his face far too close to… a specific place. She felt the moment he realized it as well because his body jolted slightly, and his tongue darted out to wet his lips.

She found herself wondering what else that tongue could do…

Now was definitely not the time!

Opening the window wider, she began to slip her arms through the gap, trying to ignore the claustrophobia that tried its best to wiggle its way to the forefront of her mind. She closed her eyes against the onslaught of information, relying on her hands and ears to guide her into the dark room beyond.

She dropped down into the space, wincing as the rim of the window dug into her hips and side. She knew she'd find an entire collection of bruises the next day, but her thoughts were stolen from her, along with her breath, when she opened her eyes to the scene before her. And a small scream broke free from her throat before she could strangle it.

Within a flash, Kingsley was next to her, his hands

on her shoulders, but he couldn't drag her attention away from the horror before her. Her people… they were… they were being cut open.

Images of bodies split from jaw to groin, insides on display, and measurements and notes hung on the walls, messy handwriting accompanying them as if they were merely the plans for a new building. So much blood everywhere, terror on the still faces of people she recognized. And her entire world felt like it was crumbling around her.

CHAPTER
THIRTEEN

Once Finley could breathe again, she pushed against Kingsley, who had shot down to his knees next to her. The things she was seeing… it wasn't just barbaric; it was downright monstrous. And Kingsley? He was part of this; he had to be in some way! He worked for the very rotten core of this godforsaken city; there was no way he could operate without being aware of this.

On the walls were photos and notes from at least fifty different vivisections, gory images of intestines and hearts laying out of place. Finley felt her stomach churn, and she gagged, but she managed to hold back the little food she had consumed today. When she felt Kingsley's hand touch her shoulder, she flinched.

"Don't," she said, not able to even meet his eyes.

"Finley, I—" he began, but she cut him off with a wave of her hand and stepped closer to the workstations. The closer she looked, the more information she collected. Each patient, each person, was documented, nearly all the people on her missing person's list. Finley swallowed, praying to whatever gods were out there that she wouldn't find her friend lying dead here also.

Trying not to look into the eyes of the people who were scattered lifeless over the desk, Finley walked toward a computer monitor. She had cataloged those who were already dead, mentally crossing their names off the list, but this was far from all who were missing. There must be a complete log of them somewhere.

Her eyes scanned the desktop for any words or files that might suggest what she was looking for, but instead, they caught onto a different word.

Test runs.

Finley didn't even blink before she started clicking on it. Her mind was whirring as she opened file after file, clicking through them, skimming the sentences. And even though she barely read all the details, what she did manage to read made her feel as if she were about to pass out. Her people were being mutilated, their bodies barraged with chemicals and physical alterations, their mouths being sewn shut while they were awake, their eyes being removed and replaced by metal stakes. The same word kept coming up again and again.

Resistant. The patient was resistant to treatment.

Her people were being cut up and modified against their will, and these sickos had the gall to call them resistant?!

She had to resist the urge to punch the monitor in front of her. As if guided by some sick need to know everything, she dug further, even though she wasn't even sure she could take any more of these sick nightmares that she couldn't seem to wake from. Videos—they had films, friends being electrocuted and injected, tied down while they fought wildly for freedom. Their screams… they were everywhere.

And Finley knew, just knew, that she wouldn't be able to banish these memories from her mind for the rest of her life. They would be etched there, alongside the crushing feeling of failure. Because she had failed; she'd failed every single one of these people. And they had paid the ultimate price.

"Finley, stop!" Kingsley's voice came from somewhere behind her, but it felt like it traveled from a thousand miles away. She didn't acknowledge him, just kept flicking through page after page, clip after clip. "Finley, please!" He sounded more insistent now, but she still blocked him out. "Finley!"

She spun around, her nails out as she rushed toward him, her sudden movement catching him off guard, and they both went tumbling to the floor. "How could you?!" She could hear herself scream, but she felt as if she were underwater, being drowned by the pressure of crushing regret. Her fists were moving, pounding into his chest again and again.

She knew he could stop her; she wasn't as strong as

him nor as clear-minded. Her hits were messy, but he took every single one, his face a tight mask of pain and something else, something she couldn't read. It felt as if the moment went on forever, on and on until her arms felt too tired to move, and her throat too raw to speak. She slumped forward over him, her shoulders shaking in quiet sobs.

"Why?" she moaned. "How could... how could anyone even—"

"I'm sorry," he whispered quietly, close to tears, but his face showed no sign of it. "There is no excuse."

"Explain this to me," she begged. "Tell me this isn't what it looks like." He remained silent, closing his eyes against the sight of her face, red-eyed and distraught.

"No!" Finley cried. "No! This can't be! Tell me you didn't! Tell me the boy I once loved isn't a murderer!"

That caught his attention, his eyes flicking open and catching hers. His face was a mask of confusion, peeking through his sorrow until it was the dominant feeling on his face. Seconds went by, and then... there. Recognition bloomed, hope, and then anger, and then... fear.

So many emotions passed over his face, and Finley reveled in the pain, the regret that coursed through him. She rolled off him, moving away.

"You're... her, the girl... from before." He sounded as if she might be a mirage, a hallucination he was scared to break.

"The girl from Earth? Yeah, Kingsley, your father shot mine, remember?" she spat, refusing to look at him.

"Finley, I—This. I can explain, please." He sounded desperate.

"Is she here?" Finley asked, ignoring his words. He halted, the silence tension with a cocktail of rotten emotions that reminded her of a stagnant pond. She repeated herself, her voice louder this time. "Damn it, Kingsley! Is she here?!"

She met his eyes, and she could see that he wanted to say no, that he wanted to tell her what she so desperately wanted to hear. But she knew as well as he did that he couldn't do that. Because Jenny wasn't just here, but she was probably dead.

"Show me!" Finley's face was expressionless now, her voice dead despite the tears that continued their constant traces down her cheeks.

He looked at his hands, clenching and unclenching them. She knew he wanted to ask her more questions, to speak to her about the secret she had just revealed, but instead, he moved silently toward the computer, clicking at the keys.

"What's her name?" he asked. They both still wanted that tiny hope that it might just be one big misunderstanding. That he hadn't done what she thought he had done.

"Jenny," she croaked, "Jennifer Rose."

Kingsley didn't pause before he started typing, then clicking, and then stepping away.

Finley couldn't even look at him as she stepped toward the screen. She held her breath, praying, hoping, pleading that she wasn't about to see what she thought she would see.

She released the breath of a ragged sob. There was

Jennifer, her name, age, and body stats. Her face, pale and lifeless, angry-looking cuts stapled back together over her chest, and a single bullet hole in the center of her forehead. She scanned the notes beneath.

The patient received v12.4 approx. 1 month before the predicted changes occurred. Successful alteration of the prefrontal cortex connections, motor function both inhibited and isolated. The patient showed increased aggression toward both humans and peers, with a successfully increased amount of muscle tone and digestive preferences. The patient is marked as: SUCCESS.

At the bottom, there was a link to a video. Finley clicked on it, and she heard Kingsley's breath catch behind her.

The room it showed was dark, and for a moment, Finley wasn't sure what she was seeing. Then a figure walked in from beneath where the camera was mounted, the same broad shoulders and dark curly hair she had become so familiar with. Kingsley stood in the room, still, his breaths steady and constant. She couldn't see his face from this angle, but she knew that if she could, she would see that his expression was as cold as ice.

Suddenly, a body shot from the shadows across the room, quick enough to make her jump. A horrifying screech came from the monitor, along with the sound of chains pulling tight. And there was Jenny, her skin a terrible gray color, her eyes bloodshot and black, her mouth and clothes covered in blood as she ferally attempted to reach Kingsley. He, on the other hand, didn't react.

She was puzzled as to why the footage was saved

when a voice came over the speakers in the video. "Commencing combat test run seventeen."

Finley closed her eyes when she heard the chains rattle to the floor as they released Jenny, hearing rather than seeing her friend rush forward to attack. She heard her wild screams, her breath panting, the sound of flesh smacking against flesh. It wasn't until a single gunshot rang out that she could bring herself to look.

Kingsley was on the floor, a gash down his arm, the other outstretched as he held a still smoking gun. One shot and bang, she was gone. He stood up and dusted himself off, and within seconds, he was once again composed. He glanced at the camera before stepping away, and the footage froze as it finished, his green eyes still staring at Finley nonchalantly from the grainy screen.

In the silence, all Finley could hear were her breath and the rushing of her blood in her ears. Out of nowhere, a siren began to blare, red lights flashing through the room. She didn't know what had triggered it, whether it was something that they did, but she couldn't really gather the interest to care. What did make her body tremor, however, was the sound of what sounded like hundreds of rabid wolves, rattling the bars of cages throughout the building. Their howls and growls were enough to make Finley shake with terror.

"Finley, we need to go!" Kingsley shouted, suddenly closer than he had been before but still not touching her. Good. She might kill him if he touched her now.

"Did you know?" she muttered.

"What—Finley, come on! We need to leave; we can

talk about this later!" He sounded frustrated, maybe even scared. For her or for himself, she couldn't tell.

His fingers touched her shoulder. She swiveled around quickly, her fingers digging into his chest. She was a good head or so shorter than him, but with her anger coursing through her, she felt bigger and meaner than ever.

"Did you know?" she demanded again, her words thick.

He swallowed, then nodded.

She couldn't breathe, couldn't be around him or any of this terrifying information. She ran for the window, somehow climbing through and away from the building. She wasn't even aware of her movements, but the next time she looked around herself, she was on the other side of the wall, on the neat roads and alleys of the upper district. All of it felt foreign and cold, like the images from the lab were following her in the shadows. Kingsley was nowhere to be seen, but she didn't stop to look.

Partly, she was glad that he was gone, because if he were here… she'd have to face him, what he'd done.

She ran blindly from the inner sanctum, wanting nothing more than to be back at home, safe in her room, curled up underneath her blanket so she could pretend, for a few minutes, that she was safe, and that nothing bad was happening.

But of course, that wasn't what happened.

About thirty minutes away from reaching her home, a net descended from above, seemingly from nowhere. In her haste, Finley's limbs tangled in the rope immediately, stumbling to the ground and grazing her hands and knees on the course concrete. She yelped, the pain burning through her, but more so her fear. She was confused, overwhelmed, and in no condition to fight.

As dark figures swarmed from the shadows, seemingly multiplying from nowhere, a weary acceptance fell over her. Maybe this was it… the end. Maybe she could finally sleep, leave this world and her failures behind. And with a deflated ego, she let the pain and exhaustion take her.

———

Finley groaned in pain as consciousness found her. Her neck ached, her shoulders burned, and her entire body felt as if she'd been jumped on by thousands of angry rats. Groggy and confused, she opened her eyes, hissing when a blinding light stung them like acid and quickly shutting them again. Giving up on sight, she tried to regain the feeling in the rest of her body, registering that her mouth was dry, and that she was tied to some sort of chair. She pulled gently on her bound limbs, holding in a cry when pain shot through them.

She froze in her struggle when she heard the murmur of voices growing closer. They entered the room, wherever that was, and quieted. She tried to keep her breathing steady and her body limp, hoping to play dead until she had a better idea of where she was and what was happening. If she had been taken by the state… she was as good as dead.

"We know you're awake, Sharpe," a leveled voice said from her side. She remained still. "You can pretend to be unconscious all night and stay on that chair, but I think we both have things we would rather be doing."

Finley sighed, lifting her head and forcing herself to open her eyes again. The light stung less this time, but her eyes still watered. She forced herself to not show her discomfort, but it was becoming incredibly harder and harder by the minute.

"Let me go!" she demanded.

The man standing before her smiled at her, his face both reassuring and evil. "There she is. I'm afraid there's no point in that. The night is gone, a new day dawn."

"What do you want with me?" she cried out, too tired to try and wiggle herself free.

"What you want, really." The man stepped forward, kneeling in front of her while several others—three men and two women—remained standing at the back of the room.

"And what is it that I want?" she asked again, attempting to bite back the words that she really wanted to say.

"To free our people," he said, and she rolled her eyes.

"Oh, great, I've been caught by a bunch of hero-eyed idiots."

The man laughed, seemingly unbothered by her insult, though his friends shuffled behind him. "Idiots, maybe, but the same could be said about you, Sharpe. Some vigilante running around like a silent protector of the poor." His words didn't sound as if they were meant to sting, but she could sense the underlying point, the hypocrisy he was trying to insinuate.

"What I do is help my friends and family survive. I don't ask them to risk their lives," Finley spat.

"All you're doing is perpetuating a faulty system," a woman from the back called out, her face so emotionless that it gave Finley chills.

"I understand that you care and worry for your people," the man in front of Finley continued. "But we want to do more than that; we want to free them, and I think, deep down, you want to as well."

"And how do you know what I want?" Finley interrogated. "You seem to know so much about me, and I don't even know your name."

He chuckled, and Finley found her interest truly piqued. Her world had been turned on its head today, and everything she thought she knew was wrong.

"My name is Hunter Cooper, and I want to help you get revenge," he said.

Against her will, a savage smile graced her face, strong enough to make her cracked lips sting.

"I'm listening."

CHAPTER
FOURTEEN

The truth hurt, and Kingsley hated that he had to tell her. But even more so, he hated that it had even happened at all. For a second, he had hope, an idea of redemption, and in less than a second, it was all gone. Blown away by his stupidity. In the end, what did he expect? He'd gotten no less than what he deserved.

He'd missed the opportunity that was right under his nose. He knew she reminded him of… her. Why wasn't he able to put it together? He had every inch of her face and voice ingrained into his mind. The idea that she could've been right in front of him, close enough to touch, and he still managed to fuck it up. Rage at himself boiled in his gut, searing his insides and making his skin tingle with frustration.

Now that he knew, he could see it in his memory of her face. He could imagine the way her childish face had morphed into the creature he saw before him. She was beautiful!

She had always been as a child, with bright eyes and soft hair. But that was the love a child had for another child, more built upon friendship and understanding. Now… she was stunning. Her face was sculpted and smooth, with high eyebrows and piercing eyes that seemed to look right through all his defenses and right to where he was most vulnerable.

And over the past few days, he had seen her face morphed and manipulated by emotions such as terror, anguish, rage, and disappointment. All. Directed. At. Him.

The pain of regret in his chest was like a familiar ocean. He was used to the way the waves lapped at him, almost drowning him completely before falling away to resurge stronger. But this time, he could feel himself crumbling away into its depths. Piece by piece, he was losing himself. He wondered if he'd even survive for much longer. He hoped he didn't.

Feeling restless and overwhelmed, Kingsley turned and did what he knew best, headed for his sanctuary. There was very little in this world that belonged to him. He was a soldier for the state, and so by definition, was owned by the state. He was merely a tool, a weapon; he had no thoughts or opinions. He only executed orders.

But still, the state couldn't forget that their mercenary ranks were built up by the sons and daughters of their wealthy people, couldn't forget that it was their blood that was spilled in the name of the higher power. So, they got some financial support. Small payments that were barely enough to survive on whenever they slaughtered someone.

The Warren was the name given to the center that housed the mercenaries, a communal living situation that was cramped at best, but decorated in a gaudy fashion that contradicted the nature of its inhabitants. There were a few common spaces, such as a recreation area with chairs and tables, places where the mercenaries could sit and talk about whose throat they cut last Tuesday.

A floor up, and there was the gym and pool, with state-of-the-art equipment to keep the soldiers in shape. But mostly, they understood that the mercenaries living in the Warren disregarded most people, including each other, and they granted each of them a room and living space, small apartments with nothing other than the bare necessities.

It had been Kingsley's only refuge. He hadn't personalized his space as many of the others had. There were no books or photos that decorated his walls. No trophies from high-value kills. If he were to die today, the only trace of him would be the sheets upon his bed and the hygiene products in his bathroom. They could throw all those away and give his room to the next mercenary within a day's turnover.

But that wasn't why his room meant so much to him. A mercenary's room was built with a biological clock, meaning that no one but the owner could enter. There were a few exceptions to the rule, however. If an overseer or state official with enough clearance wanted to gain access, they could, but that's about it. And seeing as Kingsley trusted none of his brethren as far as he could throw them, he liked knowing that he could shut himself away and remain undisturbed. Not to mention that most of his so-called allies were in fact his enemies.

The run back to the Warren was quick and easy. He was part of the inner sanctuary territory now, and his movements were rarely restricted in the area. There was a chance that there might be surveillance at the lab he'd taken Finley to, but he couldn't be bothered to worry about it now. Considering how well-guarded the inner sanctuary was, the surveillance needed on the buildings was minimal.

In the Warren, the cavernous room was dim, with low lighting in various spots to keep the space visible. Kingsley always thought it looked a little like a prison, with rows of doors going up several floors, all surrounding the communal pit. It's not completely out of the ordinary for it to be so quiet. His brethren had been trained to move quietly and efficiently, and the line between work and play often blurred. But for there to be no one around?

That was unusual. There were a lot of them, and they all worked on different schedules. The state wasn't very lax with its surveillance of the city, and there were usually groups that went out patrolling around the clock. Typically, there would always be someone coming or going, either returning from a job or heading out to one.

Tired and emotionally stunned, Kingsley tried to keep his awareness open, but all he could think about was his bed. He wanted a warm shower to loosen his tense muscles and a good night's rest. He knew he would dream of Finley, and he selfishly hoped that they would be dreams of redemption and acceptance rather than of punishment.

Did he even have a right to think about her forgiveness now? After being the one to end her friend's life, the one who took part in the experimentation upon her people?

Kingsley didn't know much of what the state was up to; he didn't even know why the men and women in the lab went as crazy as they did. But he did know that it was his people, the rich of the inner sanctum, who were behind it all.

At one point, he didn't cared. Their race was doomed, and it was more efficient if they all burned out sooner rather than later. But now, he felt like he had something to protect it for, or yet, someone to protect it for.

But was he good enough?

He was only one man, one mercenary. He was a skilled fighter, a great strategist, but the state had numbers and money on their side. No matter how good he was, he was no match against the state on his own. Just another reminder of how insignificant he was on the Planet Garwick, how insignificant he was to protect the woman he loved.

And he did love her, even after all these years. He had fallen in love with the way she moved and spoke, the determination inside of her, and her desire to protect others. She had been a mere ghost in his mind until now, but he had seen her burst to life over the past few days—even if he hadn't realized what he was seeing.

Trying not to get sidetracked, Kingsley made his way up the stairs, listening to the metal dinging beneath his booted feet. On the third floor, he exited the twisting stairs and walked the three minutes down the hall to his room. Something nagged at the back of his neck, something off, and he couldn't help the way his eyes instinctively scanned the area.

There was stillness everywhere, no movement or sound inside or out. The hairs on the back of his neck began to stand up, and he paused outside his room, his hand resting on the door handle.

He stared into the quiet air for a moment, waiting for something to happen, a strike or a trap, something that would explain the wrongness of the air around him. But everything remained desolate and empty.

Shrugging it off, he went to open his door. In the middle of pressing his weight onto the handle, a door suddenly sounded from below, and Kingsley could hear the sound of feet pounding up the stairs.

"Kingsley!" came the familiar voice of Ruby, her lithe physique appearing on the stairwell, her dark hair tossed around her flushed face. He said nothing and turned to her, watching cautiously as she came closer. Her body was tense, and her eyes also darted around the empty hall. Both of them were on edge, which confirmed to him that something was likely amiss. But instead of asking, he simply waited for her to tell him.

Would she be the savior or betrayer tonight? Perhaps that was cruel to think about after the friendship she had continuously offered to him. But he'd learned a long time ago that friendship amongst his people was never offered freely. There was always an ulterior motive behind it all. Maybe this would be the night when Ruby finally revealed hers.

As she stopped in front of him, he noticed that she was armed, her customary blades in place, and her combat clothes still on. She didn't just come from her room, which was odd because she never worked the night shift. His body stiffened as she drew closer, naturally preparing for any sort of attack.

"Thank God, I found you! You need to come with me, now!" Her voice was hurried and quiet, her body alert.

She was upset, he could tell. It was an emotion that Ruby rarely showed. When he didn't immediately move to follow her, her expression contorted with frustration, and she grabbed at his arm.

"Kingsley, this isn't a joke! I need you to come with me! Strage is on his way, and he knows that you broke into the lab with that street girl—"

Ruby's hurried explanation was cut off when Ivan appeared from the shadows further down the corridor. "It looks like a little mouse slipped through the cracks," Ivan cooed, the familiar psychopathic glint shining in his eyes.

Kingsley remained still but repositioned his body to face the bigger threat. "You know, Thompson, you had a bright future with us. Strage even planned to join your two bloodlines."

Ruby's face visibly recoiled, and she gritted her teeth. "I'd rather vomit blood than do anything with Strage."

Ivan smiled. "That can be arranged."

Suddenly, there were figures behind them, beside them, climbing up from the floors below and creeping out from the shadows. Internally, Kingsley berated himself. Usually, he was alert; an attack of this scale would've been tricky to keep hidden from him.

Now he stood at the very center of it. Reserving their energy, their mercenary training kicking in, he and Ruby allowed themselves to be bound and secured. It would take a suicidal fool to think they could free themselves from their current situation, and they had to choose their battles wisely.

Kingsley wasn't surprised when Ivans's attention shifted from Ruby to himself. "You've been a very naughty boy, Bishop. You've been playing in the gutter with the rats." Ivan spoke with such disdain that it made Kingsley's temper spark. He could take insults to himself, to his brethren and his people, but insults toward Finley were unacceptable.

"And yet, still more valuable than you," Kingsley replied, his voice deep and toneless. The malice that came naturally to him made itself known.

Ivan simply smiled more, his slightly sharpened teeth now fully showing. "You can tell that to Strage then when he cuts off your hands."

Ivan and his posse grabbed them both forcefully, using more aggression than they really needed to when their captives were cooperating. They took them from the Warren, across the inner sanctuary, and into the military building, which served as the headquarters for the state. Here, wars were planned, money was made, and lives were destroyed.

How poetic that Kingsley's own life would end here.

Throughout the compound, he saw very few people, those closest and most loyal to Strage. The rest, he gathered, must've been ordered to stay out of the way. But he was unsurprised that they had followed the order diligently. Kingsley meant nothing to any of them, his isolation truly visible now. In his twenty-six years here, he had always felt alone.

He and Ruby were dragged to the interrogation room, where they were handcuffed onto the metal chairs that usually held those considered "enemies of the state," a statement not too far off for Kingsley considering how much he despised the state.

The room was filled with more of Strage's goons, lined around the walls like dark sentinels. Strage himself stood at the center, his overly bulky body still and poised as it always was, a snake ready to strike.

He didn't smile when he saw Kingsley and Ruby, but his eyes burned with satisfaction. He said nothing as they were secured. His loyal slaves stepped away when they were done, leaving Ruby and Kingsley to Strage's non-existent mercy.

Kingsley wasn't surprised when the man took two strides forward and swung his arm, his ringed hand catching Kingsley across the jaw and causing his face to whip to the side. It made his neck ache and his jaw tingle, but he showed no reaction, his face remaining neutral. He knew that showing any sign of pain would only fuel Strage's motivation.

"Strage, this is insane! Let us go!" Ruby shrieked beside Kingsley, her usual calmness nowhere to be seen.

"We have a strict policy for treason," Ivan chirped, taking way too much pleasure from the situation. "You know that the best out of all of us, Thompson."

"I'm not a traitor, and neither is Bishop!" she spat back.

"We have proof that states otherwise," Strage said, his voice startling in the enclosed space, his pitch-black eyes tracking the pulse in her neck.

"What you're planning is crazy!" Ruby shouted again, her eyes wide.

"This has always been the plan," Strage stated. "The only thing that changed is your willingness."

"I was never willing to begin with! You're all insane. I would never do something like this—they're people, not puppets!"

"And yet, you have killed those who stood in our way and enforced the rules of our mission."

Kingsley watched as the blood drained from Ruby's face. He was disappointed, really. Had she really not known what her actions were aiding? If not, then she had been even more naïve than Kingsley had thought. But he wasn't without sympathy for the girl. She didn't deserve to be punished for what he did.

"Ruby has loyally aided the cause of the state. If someone must be labeled as a traitor, then let it be the true culprit," Kingsley spoke up, his voice cold. It caused Ivan to laugh, and Strage's attention to shift to him.

"You will be punished in due time, Bishop. But Ruby here has also participated in defying the state," Strage chanted.

"She has shown loyalty to a fellow mercenary and servant of the state. Are we no longer taught loyalty?" Kingsley shot back, and Strage gave him one of his rare and despicable grins.

"The loyalty we are taught is not to ourselves or to our ranks, nor to the preconceived ideas of what we believe the state should be. The aim of the state is as it has always been. We will continue the experiment that was started on Earth. The filths who wander the streets of Roseallan City shall convert to the mindless serfs they should've always been, and we—the worthy— shall live in paradise upon the backs of their labor."

It was a speech that Kingsley had heard as a child, the memories scattered in his dreams. He had an idea of what his people were planning, had known that it was cruel and unforgiving. But a paradise? He'd never known why they wanted the people more endangered than they already were, and now he realized that they truly were insane.

"And what about those of us who aren't turned? Shall we be consumed by them as we nearly were by the Antiqua?" Ruby snapped.

"The Antiqua were an unfortunate side effect of the early days of the experiment," Ivan explained from behind Strage. "There is a protocol to stop that from happening again."

"The only question left," Strage interrupted Ivan, glancing at him as he would a worm in the mud, "is whether you will be joining us in paradise or not.

Unfortunately, against my recommendation, you two are amongst those who must live through the second coming. You are to join us by choice or by force, whichever I deem necessary."

Kingsley's blood ran cold at the thought of his father, the monster who had been part of creating this experiment. One of the men responsible for the death and destruction of an entire planet. The filthy blood that ran through Kingsley's veins came from his father, and it would be a crime that Kingsley would always have to pay for.

Thoughts of Finley, of the little girl she had been and the strong woman she was now, swirled through his mind. If he could do anything with his meaningless existence, he could fight for her. Give to her the sacrifice she was owed, had been owed since they first met as children and his own family had torn hers apart. It would be his final redemption.

Kingsley looked up into Strage's eyes and let a smile twist from his mouth, the feeling unfamiliar and foreign.

"Over my dead body," he spat, and chaos erupted as he slipped off the cuffs that he and Ruby had silently been undoing since they arrived.

CHAPTER
FIFTEEN

Finley sat on the bed that had been issued to her by Hunter and his crew. She still didn't trust him, or any of the rebels, but she'd accepted that both their goals were somewhat linked. She wanted—no, needed —to lash back at the people responsible for the death and torture of so many of her own. Even thinking about it now, she wanted to punch at the walls until her knuckles were bloody and swollen, and her legs could hold her no longer.

Instead, she sat on the cot, her face and ribs bruised,

slowly dabbing at the cuts with the antiseptic that she had been supplied with.

Part of her wanted to return home, to her own apartment to lick her wounds and her pummeled ego. But it made more sense to remain with the rebels. No one would find her here, especially not *him*.

She had done it, told him who she was, and she didn't regret it. What she regretted was not sticking around long enough to see his face when he realized his mistake. Her anger burned for him, and she wanted to see him hurt. And if that was because his betrayal seemed to hurt more than anything else? Well, she wasn't going to draw attention to that. There was no need. Anger was anger, and she had plenty for everyone.

Where once she had dreams of peace, of living her life under the radar and existing with her people, she now wanted to see the whole city burn. She wanted to hear their screams and know that they might finally understand the suffering they'd caused her and her people. She needed them to know the extent of their mistake and wish to the gods that they could go back in time and make a different call.

It would be her pleasure to deny them that.

None of the rebels she met had apologized for the injuries they'd given her during their attack. Finley couldn't decide if she respected them or hated them for that, but it wasn't something she was going to push. She sensed that Hunter, their honorary leader, had a level head and eye for strategy. The rest of his people? They seemed less stable.

Hunter had spent some time explaining to her the

rebel force he ran and what resources they held. She was glad to see that they had a bigger reach than she'd expected, but she still didn't think they could beat the state. They had numbers on their side, but she'd seen the state's mercenaries fight, seen their cops fire their guns. They had fewer foot soldiers but better weapons.

At this stage, her people would only act as cannon fodder for a hopeless dream.

But Finley kept that judgment to herself. She would make a call as to whether she got as many people as possible out of dodge or put her weight behind this cause when the answer became clearer to her.

The rebels had people across the city, from all walks of life and in all of the sectors. She was surprised to learn that Hunter himself was from the upper class, not inner sanctuary level, but about as close as someone could get to it. He didn't explain how he'd come to support the poor and homeless, and she didn't have to ask. It was likely some heroic bullshit, something about a noble bleeding heart who couldn't bear to see others suffer. In the end, his feelings wouldn't keep her family alive.

The inner circle, as it were, had been the others who gathered in the room. It made her wonder just how many others had been invited as forcefully as she had been. It would act as a weakness later on if they had members cutting and running because the state scared them more than a bunch of maniacs in coats could ever scare them. They'd be wise to do so, and she'd advise her own people to do the same if she deemed it necessary.

The three men were introduced first, their attitudes

ranging from welcoming to disdainful. The first was a muscular ginger with a full beard and full lips. He stepped up next to Hunter with the familiarity of a lover, pulling one arm around the man. His eyes were gentle when he held out his hand.

"The name's Ezra. I'm in charge of the artillery, and I've worked closely with Jenny on some of our projects."

Just the sound of her name made Finley's chest hurt. She still couldn't believe that Jenny was truly gone. Finley would've given anything to have her by her side at this very moment, giving her strength as she always had before. She was always the ballsy one between the two of them.

Unable to speak without crying, Finley nodded, which Ezra accepted graciously, lowering his untouched hand. She didn't even bother giving him her name as they already seemed to know everything about her.

The next man to step up was much shorter, with coffee-colored skin and a thick brown handlebar mustache. His eyes gleamed, but his tone was controlled. When he spoke, he did so with an accent, which told her that he likely came from the southern parts of the old world.

"Franko. I run the bases, keep them hidden and connected. If there's a problem, you bring that shit to me," he said briskly, and she gave him another nod.

The last man to step forward was tall, almost as tall as Kingsley, and his appearance painfully reminded her of him. All the way down to the cold frown he wore like a second skin, his dark hair a straight rod down to his mid-back, a gruesome scar winding down his right eye and over to his lip, lifting it into a semi-permanent sneer. His eyes were hidden behind wide circular sunglasses that hid both his gaze and his expression. He offered no explanation for his role, only muttering "Seneca" before spinning in place and leaving.

Hunter looked at Finley with a guise that told her that her presence was the cause for his bad mood. "Seneca is our top espionage. He has spies working in the inner sanctum," Hunter explained as if it were the answer to the man's rudeness, but the mention of the inner sanctum only made her tense.

Did he know about Kingsley? The relationship they had over the last few days?

Could she even call it a relationship? They weren't friends, allies, or even acquaintances. They had been thrown together by coincidence and a bad history. Truly, there was nothing more substantial between them than mothballs and dust. Or at least, that was what she kept telling herself.

Next, the two women introduced themselves. The first one was a muscular woman around the same height as Finley, with pale blonde hair and blue eyes. She was classically beautiful, but it was hard to see past the aggression that poured off her in waves. In another world, Finley couldn't help but think she would've been someone she could have befriended; she exuded the same sort of "try me" energy that Finley often got in trouble for, and it also reminded her of Jenny.

"The name's Trench. Try not to be too much of a bitch. I run the training scheme," the woman harrumphed as if it were beneath her to speak.

Lured by her similarities to her best friend, Finley said, "She gave you a run for your money, didn't she?"

Trench stopped for a moment and froze, and for a split second, the livid air that clouded her flickered. Beneath it, Finley saw the glimmer of a woman hurting, grieving.

"The bitch was good at poker, I'll give her that," Trench said, and then the glimmer was gone, and so was she, thumping her way out the door in the opposite direction that Seneca had gone.

The last woman to come forward looked much kinder, her face soft and pretty. Her hair was an identical red to Ezra's, along with the freckles and blue eyes.

Siblings, Finley assumed.

Like her brother, she walked up to Finley, but instead of offering a hand, she went in for the full hug, embracing her stiff body despite Finley's obvious reluctance. When she pulled back, there were tears in her eyes that startled her.

She wiped at them before sniffing. "Sorry, it's an emotional time. I know Jenny's death must be heartbreaking for you. I only knew her for a short while, but she was family. I'm Bethany, by the way. I run the Pyro Department." She clapped her lightly on the back before whistling off.

Wide-eyed, Finley looked at the chirpy woman before looking back at Hunter. He simply mimicked a silent explosion with his hand and shook his head.

Right. Don't ask.

———

Later that night, he guided her to a small room and told her to rest up, this time, not tied to a chair and unconscious. He then gave her some medical supplies and disappeared.

About forty-five minutes later, Ezra appeared with some warm stew and a message to come to the next meeting at mid-day the following day. Finley didn't like that it was so far away, but she was secretly thankful. Her body was exhausted, and she wasn't sure she could put her best foot forward just yet, considering the craziness of the past twenty-four hours.

Sighing, Finley put the antiseptic wipes down on the old dresser and pulled her boots off. They felt like they were glued to her sore toes, and she winced when she freed her limbs. Once they were off, she lied back on the bed slowly, trying to ignore the way everything in her body seemed to protest. Her ribs were likely bruised, along with her spine... along with many other small but debilitating injuries. She'd live, but it would take her months to completely recover.

When she was finally lying flat, she took a moment to stabilize her breath, but the feeling of being winded only increased as the thoughts of the last few days swirled in her mind. She couldn't stop seeing images of Jenny in that room, her lifeless eyes. Then she thought about John, and then the people in that shelter who had all gone crazy. How many of her people were already dead? And how many of them were still suffering?

Unprovoked, an image of Kingsley suddenly popped up in her mind, the way his face looked when he'd tried to get her to not watch the video. The way it looked when he tried to stop her from going inside that building. He must've felt some remorse. She couldn't connect the Kingsley she had known with a man who was heartless enough to do such horrific things.

But the more she tried to humanize him, the worse she felt. She couldn't make excuses for a killer, certainly not someone who clearly held her and her own people at such low standards. Past relationship or not, she had to burn the memories of him and let him go.

Finley was so exhausted that she must've drifted off, tears slipping quietly down her cheeks and drying like salty seawater on her eyelashes. The room she was in was dark, the light outside having dropped to nothing, and a tense feeling lingered in the air. She strained her ears but heard nothing. However, she was still left with this feeling that some sort of sound had woken her from her shallow sleep.

Slowly, she lifted herself from the cot; her muscles ached more than they had before, but she could tell they were less fragile. She then quietly walked over to the door, not bothering with her boots seeing that her socked feet on the floor were much quieter.

Silently, she slipped through the door and into the wooden hallway. The rebel's building was a re-creation of an old Japanese-style home, with paper hatched walls and wooden walkways surrounding an inner garden that the building wrapped around.

Finley walked up to the railing and peered into the empty garden below, her eyes scanning the neatly trimmed bushes and trees. The water then rippled gently in the breeze, and small bugs skated across its surface. Everything was still, so still.

Too still.

Figures rapidly exploded from the room behind her, tearing the paper door apart as they rolled onto the grass, moving so fast that Finley could barely see where one ended and the other began. It wasn't until another one joined the scuffle, Trench, that they stilled long enough for her to identify them as Seneca and... Kingsley.

Except it almost didn't look like Kingsley, not beneath the cuts and blood and swelling skin. Instinctually, something pulled in her core, and Finley found herself running before she could even register it, running to him. To Kingsley. To make sure he wasn't hurt.

When she flew into the garden, the two men, who were still trying to reach each other with flailing arms, were being pulled apart. Seneca looked even more enraged than he had been earlier, his eyes wide and rolling like some crazed beast.

"Stop this now!" Hunter roared as he stormed from the building opposite them, his dark coat flying behind his legs. The men stilled in their captor's arms, enough so that Ezra—who had been holding Seneca—let him go and straightened his posture.

Seneca, no less angry but seemingly more in control, spat, "A filthy mercenary spy."

"The black kettle said to the pot," Finley muttered, regretting it when all eyes shifted to her—including Kingsley's.

"Do you know this mercenary?" Hunter then asked her, his eyes serious and with no trace of the welcoming warmth she had sensed earlier. This was a leader keeping his troops safe from anyone who sought to hurt them.

"In a sense," Finley replied, not really knowing how to phrase it.

"Who cares if the bitch knows him?! We should kill him now and spare ourselves the risk!" Seneca cried.

"Don't call her a bitch, you traitor," Kingsley snarled from his place in Trench's arms, pulling but failing to set himself free. If things weren't so chaotic, Finley could've sworn she saw his legs shake, but she was distracted from the thought when Seneca whirled toward Kingsley again. Ezra stepped forward as if he's about to grab the man, but stopped when Seneca kept his distance.

"I'm a traitor?! She's dead because of you! She was worth more than the dirt that covers your boots, and yet you are here, and she's not!" Within seconds, Seneca's expression was crumpling, and tears began to run down his angular face.

It was only then that Finley realized his sunglasses were gone, and she could see his pale gray eyes. But it was a minor observation when the man started sobbing on the floor.

Hunter stepped up to him, crouching to place a comforting palm on his back. Seneca didn't even flinch, just kept digging his fingers deeper into the ground. It was then that Hunter's eyes flicked over to Finley.

"Figure out what the hell is going on, or I'll kill the mercenary tonight."

Finley gulped and nodded, not knowing why she wasn't just telling him to slit Kingsley's throat. He deserved it after everything he'd done. Except when she looked over to him, into his eyes that were bruised and puffy, she just found herself looking at that same boy she'd known when she was younger. She didn't know what she was going to do, but she knew she wasn't quite done with Kingsley just yet.

CHAPTER
SIXTEEN

Trench was the one who manhandled Kingsley down to the cells. She was smaller than him, but her strength, combined with how exhausted he looked, meant that he was mostly deadweight. And in Trench's arms, that looked about as difficult to carry as it was to carry a plate from one surface to the next.

Finley told herself she was glad to see blood dripping from his mouth and smeared over his teeth, that she liked the way it looked, staining his skin. But despite all that, she still felt her heart beat whenever his head lulled too far, or whenever his feet tripped on the ground, and he lurched a little too erratically.

Stupid traitorous heart.

When Trench dumped her old friend unceremoniously into a cell and swung the metal barred door shut, caging him in, Finley didn't wince. She wasn't sure if her heart was committed to his death as of yet, but her mind was certainly angry, and she didn't feel it was wrong that he received a bit of rough handling.

She understood he'd been alone for most of his life, trapped with a father who was cold as ice and surrounded by people much the same. She could forgive him for his emotional liability. But what she couldn't seem to forgive were his actions, the things he'd done without a flinch or a frown. How could he be anything but a monster?

And that was what terrified her the most. Finley thought she'd been secretly in love and pining for a terrible creature all these years, that the last bit of hope left in her was being fizzled out for good. Selfish, really. But growing up the way she did, no one else had her back. If she didn't care about herself, no one would.

Trench shot Finley a look as she walked past, her blonde brows raised in question. With no answer to give, Finley simply dipped her head, her body remaining tense until the other woman left. Above her, she could still hear footsteps, the murmur of raised voices as they struggled to calm themselves from the outbreak earlier.

She was still focusing on the movement upstairs when Kingsley appeared by the bars beside her, so quiet that it made her jump back a step.

Up close, she could see the true damage done to him. His cheeks were bruised as well as his eyes, the skin swelling and blotchy. His lips and brow were both cut, and his hair was so unkempt that it looked as if someone had tried to drag him by it.

Unable to stop herself, she found her eyes traveling down his body, scanning for more injuries. She bit her lip when she found several places where he looked like he had been cut by something sharp, gaps in his leather uniform revealing bloody skin. He also looked like he was putting all his weight on his right leg, his left lifted and loose—likely a dislocated knee.

Her instinct was to go to him, run her fingers across his skin to check that he was in fact still real, not some life-like figment of her lonely mind. Instead, Finley settled for a glare, refusing to be the first one to speak when her internal monologue was so scattered.

Kingsley stood there, still towering over her despite his battered form, a look in his eye that was ghostly enough so that it made a shiver skitter down her spine. When they held each other's gaze for what felt like several moments, he seemed to deflate, his large body sliding down the rough wooden wall until he was sitting by the bars and looking up. It was from this position that Finley felt strange, looking down at a man she had been so used to gazing up to. It felt both empowering and terrifying, and in a strange combination, she wanted to run from him and to him.

When the silence became too tense, Finley finally broke. "What are you doing here?" she asked, but it was less of a question and more of a statement. Her voice didn't carry the bite she had wanted it to, and instead, she just sounded sad.

He broke eye contact for the first time in minutes and looked down at his fingers, which were red and smudged with drying blood. "I...," he began, but his voice cracked as if too sore to speak.

She waited for a moment, but when it looked like he wasn't going to continue, she sighed in frustration. "You know what? Fuck this! Fuck this, and fuck you, Kingsley. You've been treating me like shit for the last few days, and I'm done with it all. I'll let them fucking slit your throat. You might even say more that way!" Finley yelled, stomping in the direction of the door. Her hand was on the knob when she heard his voice, cursing herself for the way she immediately stopped.

"Wait," he finally said, barely above a small whisper. "Please, Finley, I-I don't know what to say. What can I say that would make this better?"

She spun to look at him. "To make this better?! There is nothing you can do, Kingsley, to make the fact that you killed one of my closest friends better! Maybe show some goddamn regret for once!"

Kingsley was up in a flash despite his injuries. "Regret?!" he retorted angrily. "My whole life has been nothing but regret! I did what I had to do to survive!" He paced around the small cell before coming back to meet her eyes. "And while we're on the subject of blame, why didn't you tell me who you were when we met? You lied to me!"

Finley scoffed. "Because I couldn't trust you! You work for the fucking government now, and it's in your nature to kill those like me."

"Kill you?!" He looked genuinely shocked. "Finley, I would never purposely hurt you. You need to know that."

"You already have." She sighed, feeling an ache bloom in her chest. She wanted so badly to be able to push it all aside and just enjoy having found him. She wished she could go back in time and wipe away all his wrongdoings. "What have you gotten yourself into?" Her voice cracked with emotion.

He shot back to the bars at the appearance of water in her eyes, reaching toward her and almost growling when he couldn't. "Please, Finley, I'm so sorry."

"That's not good enough!" she cried. "You've pushed me around over the past few days, following me while I tried to figure out what was going on with my people, my friends, and you said nothing! I must've looked so stupid! Were you laughing? Was it fun for you to watch me flail for someone who was already gone?"

"No!" he shouted back. "I just… I didn't know what to say, what to do. I just wanted to keep you safe, however I could!"

"Ha!" She laughed sarcastically. "Of course, of course, you'd want to protect me by keeping me in the dark, telling me absolutely nothing, and letting me flounder. How silly of me to have misread that! You obviously had great intentions."

"Please, let me explain. I need you to understand," he begged.

But his pleading just enraged Finley even more. "It's too late, Kingsley."

"Just listen," he begged again, his voice jumping

when she turned toward the door. "Listen to what I have to say, and if you still hate me, you can go. Let me rot down here and die, but I need you to hear me out."

She observed him for a second, unsure of what to do. He looked different than he did before, the icy exterior gone. Instead, she saw a young man, a desperate and tortured young man. And for the first time, she could see the imprint of her childhood friend in him. And because of that, she sat down and nodded her head.

As Kingsley explained, which he did in painfully specific detail, Finley said nothing. She neither acknowledged that she was listening nor made it obvious that she wasn't. Remaining impartial like a coast getting battered by the stormy shore. She felt her chest tighten as he explained the experiments that began on Earth and led to the Antiqua outbreak, the re-colonization of the new planet, and the plans to continue with the experiments.

And finally, how the vaccine was the state's way of infecting all its citizens so they would become the next generation of mindless slaves. It was terrible and heartbreaking to hear. Kingsley had seen and done horrific things, things that made even Finley's stomach churn.

When he was done, they were silent for a moment, nothing but the sound of them breathing in the damp air of the cell.

When she finally spoke, it felt too loud in the tense room, as if it were disturbing something sacred and delicate.

"Ruby, she was the black-haired mercenary I saw on

the first day?" Finley asked, not looking at Kingsley despite the fact that his gaze was glued to her.

"Yes," he responded.

"And she is…"

"Dead? Also, yes."

"And she died helping you escape your brethren, who were trying to force you into the scheme?" It all felt too insane, and Finley could tell that her expression echoed that.

"Yes," Kingsley said yet again, and she could detect genuine regret in his voice. "She was in a relationship with Seneca, and that's why her death hurts him so much."

Finley nodded her head but said nothing. She didn't know what to say. The things Kingsley had grown up around would poison even the most innocent of minds, and the fact that he was still fighting the system to this day was admirable. But her heart still pained for the loss of her friend, and so many whom she considered family.

"I don't know how to forgive you, even after hearing all this," she whispered, a single tear trailing down her cheek. "I want to. I've missed you for so long, and it breaks my heart to know what you've been through, but you took my best friend from me. I feel like I'm being torn in half."

Kingsley reached a finger out toward her through the bars, moving slowly to allow her to move away if she wanted to. When she didn't, he carefully pressed his finger to the tear, wiping it away with the gentle touch of a feather.

"You don't have to forgive me," he murmured back,

enthralled by her close presence. "Just give me a chance to show you that I can be better, that I'm already better just having been beside you for a few days. Let me redeem myself, to you and to myself."

She closed her eyes at his words. She didn't know if she could accept them. Her emotions screamed at her to take it; she could both have him and never forgive him. But the other part of her was filled with doubt.

But then she thought back to Seneca, to his face and the pain displayed there from the death of his partner. Finley never knew Ruby, but she seemed like a good woman, and she was sorry for Seneca's loss. His love was well and truly gone, in a place where he couldn't reach her. Whereas Finley's love was right in front of her, reaching out and begging for her to accept him. Would she be a fool to turn him down? So little happiness was guaranteed in their world. Was it not time to claim her own fortune?

Decision made, she opened her eyes, unsurprised to see his emerald green ones watching her with bated breath. She couldn't help the small smile that graced her lips, and his own face reacted immediately. He looked as if he'd just laid eyes on a beautiful gemstone; the way his face lit up made her blush instantly.

"I can try," she murmured.

And then she leaned forward, rejoicing inwardly when she felt his soft lips touch her own. It felt like coming home to a family, as warmth spread throughout her body. She reveled in the way his lips moved against her own, like some sort of primal dance that only their hearts knew.

When she pulled away, she was breathless despite

its chastity, and she could tell Kingsley was as well. She smiled at that again, and this time, she thought her eyebrows would lift into her hairline.

"What?" she asked, embarrassed.

He chuckled back, the sound warm and inviting. "I just love the way you smile."

"Yeah, well, then I guess you better make it happen more," she huffed, standing up and walking to the keys hanging on the wall.

She then unlocked Kingsley's cell doors and tried not to let herself tremble with nerves. They had just kissed, so she shouldn't be nervous. But something about him being right there in front of her, able to reach her, made her insides feel like jelly.

She thought she might even swoon when he stepped into her body heat and cupped her cheeks in his large, rough palms.

"You'll never know tears again, I promise," and for some reason, probably a stupid one, she believed him.

When they went back upstairs, they did so hand-in-hand, the warmth of his body seeping into Finley's and filling her with hope. Her new rebel friends were surprised when they saw them together, and she had to stop Hunter from stabbing him on the spot, explaining to them the information Kingsley had shared with her and how they could use him to help stop it all. They seemed hesitant at first, and Seneca was nowhere to be seen, but Finley put forward a convincing front, telling them about how Kingsley had gotten her into the inner sanctum

But she didn't leave out his sins, explaining all the ways he had betrayed them and their people for many years, but she also told them how willing he was to now help their cause.

She didn't think they'd accept her argument. She hadn't known them long, and one of their own had suffered a brutal loss because of Kingsley, so she was surprised when Hunter stepped forward and clapped Kingsley on the back. An emotion that was obviously shared by Kingsley from the wide-eyed look he gave her.

"This is our last chance," Hunter stated, his voice hypnotic and motivating. "We strike now, and we strike hard, for freedom!" He cheered, and everyone around him followed suit, letting the intoxicating feeling of nerves and hope mix into their blood and fill them with foolish hope.

Foolish hope that would end up being so very false.

CHAPTER
SEVENTEEN

The plan had been steadfast, Finley was sure of it. She was usually a strategic person—though it wasn't something she'd demonstrated well over the past few weeks. It had been mind-boggling how busy it could be planning a rebellion.

She hadn't known the Core long and immediately caused a disturbance by having Kingsley follow her, but they were accepted into the ranks alarmingly well. The Core were good people, really, and she felt bad for having insulted them in the past. But now that she was involved, now that their cause was her cause, she was eager to make sure they were successful. With how rapidly the state's plans seemed to be escalating, she knew they didn't have much time.

They had built their own defenses, stocked up with food and weapons, and made sure their people were as prepared to fight as possible. But still, it was daunting. They were trying to pierce the heart of the city, and none of them could even begin to guess what the consequences would be.

In the end, they all agreed that their first mission was to free those being tested from the labs. The state would only continue to get stronger the more soldiers they turned into Antiqua, and the Core was in danger of being completely outnumbered.

The first thing they did was spread the word across the underground channels to stop getting the vaccine, and if people had already received it, they were to lock themselves in a safe place or come to the Core to be secured.

Over fifty people had come to them in the past week, scared and looking to be saved, and it hurt Finley physically that she was unable to help them. She could try and keep them from hurting themselves or anyone else, but as far as a cure went, she was clueless.

Each of Hunter's main disciples had a specific target area where they could influence. Trench worked with the engineers who kept the city running. Ezra ran into the higher societal rings with Hunter, and Bethany had connections with the medics throughout Roseallan City. Franko knew a lot of the working class, and even Seneca was handy in carefully gathering those from within the mercenary band to help support them—one of which was Kingsley.

Finley's relationship with Kingsley continued to blossom since their kiss down in the cell, and things were certainly getting heated between them. However, there was still bad blood between them, and there were still so much about each other they had yet to learn after all these years apart. To go any further felt like a step that was just too big to take. For now, they were content just sharing a bed, and Finley secretly loved curling up to Kingsley's warm body at night. It helped her feel safe during a time when her world was unstable.

When game day arrived, everything seemed fine. All their equipment were prepped and ready, and everyone was present and alert. The tension between Seneca and Kingsley was still high, Seneca refusing to look or talk to Kingsley, but as long as they could work together without killing each other, the group was secure.

Finley had come to realize that the Core had many skilled soldiers, all with good minds and reasonable goals. What she had first thought were a bunch of lunatics trying to drag her people into a battle that wasn't worth fighting, were now an impressive and reliable team of fighters who could potentially save her and the rest of the planet.

They left in the early hours of the day, when the human's body rhythm was naturally at its lowest. It would make the guards sluggish and slow to respond, and it would make moving without being seen much easier.

The Tack Room, the room that housed the equipment and weapons, was silent as they all geared up, filled with noises of clips fastening and barrels sliding. There was tension shared between all of them, one of hope and dread alike. They knew they could die tonight, and while some of them were seasoned fighters —like Trench and Hunter—there was still a risk that came with heading out.

Jokes had no place in a room like this.

Finley stepped over to Kingsley once she was dressed in the dark black camo outfit that had been provided to all of them, quietly strapping on a handgun and several knives. Finley didn't feel comfortable around the handiness of a gun. She'd been at the wrong end of it too many times to count, but she couldn't help but still be jumpy around it.

She'd be a fool not to carry one tonight, but she also made sure to bring many blades, something she'd been familiar with her whole life.

Kingsley's outfit was similar to his old mercenary uniform, which had also been thick, black leather. These clothes, however, were looser, and somehow looked more casual on him.

A part of Finley expected his mask to fall back into place after Ruby died. She had a sneaking suspicion that it'd been the adrenaline and shock of the night that led him to be so expressive, but every day since, he continued to surprise her with emotions. Where once she had fought hard to even get a glimpse of what he was feeling, she now had offered to her freely, always on display for her to see. It made her feel closer to him, which on its own, was a miracle.

When she approached him, and he looked up, she felt her stomach twist in the way it always did when a small smile graced his plush lips, but then he lowered it when he saw her serious expression.

"You okay?" he asked, though the question was redundant. They both knew she wasn't.

"I—" she hesitated, wondering if this was too much to reveal. But his gentle hand on her arm prompted her to continue. "I want to know what to do if we get separated," she said, her eyes searching his face for some sort of reaction.

What she received was a frown. "Separated? Finley, that's not going to happen. I won't let it—"

"Don't," she interrupted. "Don't pretend like we have control over that sort of thing. I lost you once before, and I don't want to lose you again. So, tell me, what should I do if we get separated?"

He looked at her for a moment, assessing her as if she had baffled him in some way. "Stubborn woman," he murmured, leaning down to kiss her lips across his own. "If we get separated, we meet back at your apartment. No one knows where it is except for us, right?"

She nodded, agreeing with the plan. "And if one of us is captured?"

He sighed. "Finley, please, I—"

"If one of us is captured, we move forward with the plan. No crazy rescue missions or sacrifices," she cut in again stubbornly.

"I can't agree to that," he whispered. "I'll need to come after you."

"But if it were you who was captured? Would you want me running into the line of fire?"

"No, but I'm different. I've done things I need to pay for; you deserve to keep going."

"No, Kingsley. I can't have that. You promise me you won't come after me if I'm captured, or I swear, I'll come after you if you get taken away." Finley could see the way he struggled internally when she said that, trying desperately to find a loophole. But eventually, he just nodded and agreed.

They were going to battle today, likely the first of many, and their future was by no means guaranteed. They had to be realistic about what was going to happen.

After their talk, they went and joined the rest of the crew, packing up the jeeps with equipment, then splitting into their assigned groups. There would be three stages to the heist. The first group, Group A—which comprised of Hunter, Trench, and Seneca—would enter the inner sanctum and the lab beyond, freeing the ones who'd been kidnapped.

They would then be guided by the second group, Group B—which comprised of Franko, Kingsley, and Ezra—who would help the subjects across the wall and into the arms of the final group, Group C.

Bethany and Finley were in the last group, both chosen for the fact that they knew the sewer system well and could navigate in the dark. They were also the smallest of the crew and would blend in along the outskirts of the city while guiding the refugees toward the safe house set up in the Hopeless District.

They also had many supporters who would wait in

the sewers to guide the people to the right place, and a recovery crew on the other side to care for those who were injured, but only the main members of the Core would put themselves in harm's way with the enemy. And if anything were to go wrong, they would disperse immediately. There were no martyrs in this heist. Every one of them would run as if their lives depended on it. Having a few remain to fight another day seemed like a much better consensus than going down all at once.

The drive to the wall was done in silence, the heaviness of the task ahead weighing upon their shoulders, and when the time came to split up, there were no hugs or tearful farewells. One minute, they were side-by-side, and the next, Finley and Bethany were tucked into an alley by a sewer entrance. Watching and waiting for figures to come across the wall.

It took about an hour, but after a while, the first few people skirted across, climbed over sections of the wall after Seneca and Hunter had taken down the surveillance cameras. The people who came to them—two young boys and an older woman—looked haggard and pale, their eyes wide but unseeing.

Finley shivered when Ezra handed them over to Bethany. She wanted to run out and kill those who had done such horrible things to the innocent, but there was no time for that, no room for her feelings of fury. Instead, she took the woman by the elbow and guided her firmly to the sewer entrance, waiting for Bethany to climb down before she handed over the rescued.

Finley held her breath for a moment after the first batch had gone into the darkness beneath the city, waiting for an alarm to wail or guns to fire and kill them instantly, but she continued to wait patiently until the next batch of three were brought to her—this time, two women in their forties and a little girl—and still, there were no disturbances. Nothing moving in the night but their own.

———

Two hours in, and Bethany had moved to the bottom of the ladder permanently to make the process of moving those they rescued quicker. Finley couldn't help but feel vulnerable all alone, so exposed in the belt around the wall where no homes or buildings resided. And when Ezra waved a hand to signal that the lab was cleared, she couldn't believe it! She was so sure that something would go wrong, but when she saw that flag, all she wanted to do was grab Kingsley and relish in their victory.

Silently, she signaled down to Bethany that the lab was cleared, and that she was to retreat back to the warehouse, shutting and sealing the entrance as if they had never been there. Looking up at the wall, Finley could no longer make out the dim figures she had seen moving around earlier, but they were the least of her concerns now.

She quickly grabbed the remaining equipment that she could find and began jogging back to safety, another bit of tension releasing when she entered back into the densely populated jungle of buildings. But she knew she wouldn't be truly relaxed until she was back at the Core's warehouse and in Kingsley's arms.

Maybe tonight, she'd take things a little further with him, celebrate in both mind and body.

Suddenly, she felt something hit her shoulder, propelling her body forward with the momentum of her speed, and knocked her over onto the concrete pavement. The pain was so blinding that she couldn't quite pinpoint what was happening. It felt as if her entire shoulder was burning, her muscles up in flames and tearing apart at the seams.

Her cry of pain was choked in her throat when a figure dropped down on top of her, a hand ringing around her next and cutting off her circulation. She scrambled, swinging her arms wildly to try and reach for one of her blades, but whoever was on top of her was much bigger and stronger, and soon, everything turned dark.

———

When Finley awoke, she did so startlingly, her body jolting to life. Immediately, her shoulder sizzled with pain, the injury making her wince. She turned her head to look at it but was distracted by the metal bolt impaling her when she realized where she was. She was strapped to a surgical table in a dark room with reflective walls. She could see herself on the ceiling, the way her eyes bugged from her face, and her legs fought uselessly to break free from her binds.

It was a moment that was only made worse when she heard a familiar laugh.

"So, you think you could get away with all our patients?" the voice cooed maliciously. "I told you I'd skin you, you little bitch, and I always pay out on my promises." Ivan Richards shoved his face into hers, his rancid breath washing across her face and his wild eyes wheeling.

Looking into their blue depths, Finley finally understood that she was no longer dealing with a man. Ivan was a monster, a creature crazed for blood and pain. So, she did the only thing she could think to do in that moment; she spat in his face.

He smiled, then backhanded her, a ring she hadn't known he was wearing catching her above the brow and cutting her skin. She could feel her blood trickling down the side of her face, which now tingled with warmth.

"Oh, I'm going to have so much fun making you scream," he hollered, prancing over to a table she couldn't quite see and rustling around with something that sounded like steel.

When he turned back around with a blade and a pair of industrial tweezers, Finley felt her stomach tighten and turn, bile threatening to make its way from her ragged throat. Unwilling to break, to give him the satisfaction of her fear, she made herself smile her most boastful and arrogant grin.

"Give me your worst," she spat again, then she closed her eyes and pictured Kingsley, her sweet, sweet Kingsley—who would be somewhere now, wishing he had never made the promise that he had.

But she found comfort in knowing that he wouldn't come for her, that he wouldn't put himself at risk. The people she loved were safer than they had been yesterday, and in that, she had accomplished what she'd always wanted.

And when she heard Ivan's boots approaching her, she let herself drift away, floating on the memories of a shattered past so far away that it almost seemed like a fantasy. She thought of her mother, her father, and the comfort of the family she knew she once had. So wrapped up in her thoughts that she didn't even feel anything when he began to cut.

And when it finally broke through, she began to scream, and tears pooled in her eyes, but still, she held on. He could break her body, tear her apart from limb to limb, but he would never be able to break her spirit.

CHAPTER
EIGHTEEN

Kingsley was furious! Three days. For three days, she'd been missing, and in that time, he couldn't stop himself from pacing, obsessing, and searching for her. He knew he'd made a promise, but he didn't care. Nothing mattered more to him than finding her… dead or alive.

He felt a stab of pain shoot through his chest at the thought of her death, the horrible image of her body lifeless and limp.

Where was his calm and collected self now? He'd

always prized it over everything else; it helped him find his way out of any situation despite the odds. When others panicked, lost their heads, and scrambled into mistakes, he took the high road. He examined everything cautiously and made calculated decisions. He needed that now. He needed to be able to *think*.

But every breath, every movement, was filled with his nightmares, nightmares of Finley's screams, her cries, her tears. Tears welled in his eyes until he couldn't even recognize his own reflection anymore.

Shaking his head, he ran faster down the streets, past the homeless and poor who inhabited the Hopeless District. They were familiar with him now, and he recognized the same faces every day when he ran that same route, searching every corner of this godforsaken city for any sign of Finley.

The people he went past knew her, were her family, and he both loved and hated them for sharing that connection with her. They had kept her safe when he hadn't, couldn't. They had been her support and given her the strength she had today. But they also had time with her, years and years of it that Kingsley had missed out on. And he'd be damned if he didn't make up for that lost time. She wasn't gone. He wouldn't allow it.

He rounded the next corner without paying attention; his muscles knew how to steer him on this course. He could run it with his eyes closed, did it in his sleep every night, aching over every detail in case he had missed anything at all.

He tried to get in contact with someone inside the sanctum, which had been locked down since the raid. The inner barrier was locked, and no one had been allowed to come and go since. The cops in the city tripled, each of them carrying large guns and batons. But they hadn't found any trace of the rescued patients, and they wouldn't.

Everyone rescued was safely being cared for by the Core, rehabilitated by volunteers from the Hopeless District, hidden in areas that the rich knew little about. Kingsley was sure the police force would come away empty-handed.

But that didn't change the fact that the patients had still been experimented on, infected with the vaccine. He had only been around them the night of the rescue, when he still thought Finley was safe. He'd walked amongst them and seen their empty eyes, their faces forever marked by pain and terror. Some of them were mute, still as if their soul had left their body behind long ago. And others were perpetually moving, mumbling as if being in their own skin hurt them.

But Kingsley didn't blame them. Some of the mutilations were… he couldn't even give a name to what he felt when he saw them.

And then there was the issue regarding the madness that took over every night. Kingsley had been privy to some of the discussions surrounding the experiment, but he didn't know everything about it. He knew the vaccine was designed to turn the population into a mindless army of servants who could neither disobey nor think for themselves.

The first attempt had produced the Antiqua, flesh-eating creatures that didn't sleep or stop until their head was detached from their body. This version, however, had been devastatingly more successful.

Those infected with the successful variant of the virus didn't move during the day. They sat comatose, neither eating nor drinking. Their bodies could wither, bleed or fester, and still, they wouldn't budge. And when ten rolled around at night, they would shatter to life. If it could even be called that anymore.

When the receptors in their brain were activated by the lack of ultraviolet light—the sun sinking fully at ten every night on Garwick—their aggression was turned on, their inhibitions turned off along with any form of empathy or impulse control.

Inside, they were awake, conscious. But their body was no longer theirs to control, a slave to the re-wired chemicals in their brain. They attacked everything in sight, each other, the uninfected. They weren't hungry for flesh like the Antiqua, only hungry for violence.

The patients too far gone were locked up in cells for their own protection. Some of the members of the Core suggested they be put down, like an animal with an incurable injury. And to an extent, Kingsley agreed. These people would only be perpetually hurting, and as far as he knew, there was no cure for them. No relief except in death.

But he also knew Finley would never allow it. She would protect every single one of them until she couldn't anymore. And so, in her absence, he kept them alive, locked up, and as safe as they could possibly be.

Kingsley, in his own desperation, had even approached Seneca, who'd sworn to gut him if he ever tried to speak to him again. The man was still grieving over the death of Ruby, something Kingsley could sympathize with. And in any other circumstance, he would've respected the man's wish.

But these weren't normal times, and he'd rather risk his life trying everything he could to find Finley.

To his surprise, Seneca had expected him. The man hadn't even raised an eyebrow when Kingsley approached him at the bar in the common room of the Core's base.

"I need you to get me back inside," he said with no preface, clenching his jaw when Seneca said nothing in reply, instead, taking another deep sip of his whisky.

Kingsley found himself closing in on enough rage to break through the dry wall when Seneca finally spoke, his eyes unreadable from beneath his black glasses.

"I can't," was all he said, and then took another swig.

"You don't understand! I need to get back in. I need… I need to find her," Kingsley pleaded, begging for Seneca to not punish Finley for Kingsley's wrongdoings.

"You misunderstood me," Seneca explained, his voice rough and his face turning grim. "I no longer have connections within the sanctum. Since the lockdown, all my spies have either been slaughtered or have abandoned the cause. They're purging on the inside; no one who isn't an unwavering supporter is allowed to live." He downed the rest of his drink, signaling to the bartender for more. "You'd be shot on sight," he finished.

Kingsley had heard stories of Seneca amongst the mercenaries. He'd been one of the sanctum's best until he'd gone rogue, rebellious, and disappeared before the state could dismiss him. He had great respect for the man, but Kingsley could tell that Ruby's death broke him. He would be of no help in this condition.

The memory brought back the same frustrated rage in Kingsley now. His body felt as if it were on fire even as the cold morning air battered his face. Nothing made sense anymore, and he couldn't find his footing any more than he could fix the mess his people had made.

With his body heaving and exhausted breaths, Kingsley bolted out of the building and didn't stop until he reached the furthest point of the city, allowing his body to collide with the final city wall, the harsh thud of flesh on brick. The pain ricocheted through his bones, and he reveled in it, a small reprieve from the constant ache in his heart.

From here, he'd usually run back to the Core's base, re-checking the alleys and paths for the slightest clue. He ran the route three times a day, and every time, he found nothing.

Today seemed as if it would yield the same results, when he noticed a gathering of people along the wall's barrier. They were a small bustling group, around ten of them based on what he could see, and they seemed to be looking at something on the ground.

Dread filling him, Kingsley sprinted toward them, ignoring the way his muscles protested against the idea. Every foot closer to them was both euphoric and damning. Would he find her? Would he finally be able to hold her in his arms again? Would she be dead? Would she be worse than dead?

When he got to the group, they noticed him immediately, parting like the Red Sea and revealing a slumped form on the gravel. His heart jumped into the back of his throat when he recognized her dark hair, matted with blood and grime. He knew the form of her body, even when her limbs were bent and broken.

The air he breathed felt like fire, and it scorched him from the inside out. One of the young men who had been part of the group spoke up timidly.

"We only just found her," he said, his face downcast. "We were gonna try to clean her up before we called you."

Kingsley couldn't bring himself to respond. He didn't know if his words would come out like a cry of pain or a roar of anger. And so, he kept it all locked inside, swirling together like a tornado. He took a few steps toward the body and stopped again, suddenly not sure if he could do this. If he could bear it.

The boy, the same one who had spoken, shook subtly next to him, the tremors almost imperceptible. He was trying to keep on a brave face for those around him, but he was as heartbroken by this as Kingsley was. Kingsley reached a hand out to the boy, and the boy flinched as if he expected him to hit him. As if he were to blame for all this.

When Kingsley's hand landed gently on the boy's shoulder, he looked up at him with wide eyes. Still, Kingsley couldn't summon words, but he shook his head, silently willing the boy to understand.

It's not your fault. Don't carry the burden of this death when it's mine to lift.

Kingsley knew the boy had received some extent of his message when he burst into tears, his shuddering breaths too large for his thin form. The boy cared for

Finley, he knew. And he realized then that her death wouldn't only be his heartbreak, but her community's as well.

Bracing himself, he forced his feet to make the final steps toward the shattered body. He knelt and gently pushed her hair from her face. His breath caught in his throat when he saw her features. A part of him, deep down, had still been clinging onto the hope that it wasn't her. That he'd uncover the body's face and find that it was only someone of similar build and stature.

A ringing began in his ears as he slid his hands under her body and felt her cold weight as he lifted her to his chest. She felt so light and fragile in his hands. Her skin was pale, too pale, enough so that it almost looked transparent, her blue and purple veins too visible on her cheeks and eyelids.

Her lips were blue and pulled down into a frown, and her body was covered with blood. Kingsley couldn't bring himself to look at the extent of her wounds, to register the way her arm bent in the wrong place or how her neck was skewing at the wrong angle. A single cut marred her brow, dried blood still showing the trail it took down her face, carving up her features as harshly as any blade could.

Kingsley felt hollow when he looked at her, and it only got worse when he began the long, slow trek back to the Core. He couldn't sense or feel anything past her, taking steps without realizing where he was going, breaths prolonging a life he didn't want.

He was vaguely aware that as he walked, people joined him. The small group that had found her body slowly grew from ten to twenty to forty. By the time

Kingsley reached the base, hundreds of heads behind him hung in sorrow.

It felt as if the world was somehow more fragile now, like glass surrounding him ready to shatter. Outside the Core's building, Hunter and his council greeted them with shuttered looks. They hadn't known Finley as long as the rest had. But even in the short time they've worked with her, they had come to respect her.

Kingsley thought Seneca put a hand on his shoulder as he walked past, but he didn't stop to check. He didn't care. He walked into the building and down to the infirmary in the basement. Laying her out on the metal table with a care that didn't even matter anymore.

He hated how still she was, how quiet. Finley had been full of life, of fight. Always vibrating with energy. Now… she looked more like a poorly rendered statue of herself. It was disgusting!

Kingsley wasn't sure how long he stared at her body. He thought people might've come and gone, but he didn't move, and he didn't look away. And when exhaustion finally took him, dragging him into unconsciousness, he still saw her. Her dead cloudy eyes looked up at him with accusation.

Why didn't he stop this?

And why didn't he save her?

CHAPTER
NINETEEN

Pain.

That was the first thing Finley felt. It was everywhere. All-consuming. It was the blood in her veins, and the breath in her lungs. She wasn't sure she even had a body anymore. Maybe she was an entity, a formless mass of writhing agony. The idea was only reinforced when she tried to open her eyes and couldn't. They seemed to be sewn shut, her lids sticking together and searing. She tried to move her fingers next.

Nothing. Her toes? Nope. When she couldn't even seem to twitch her face, she began to panic.

She was awake. Alive. But her body was dead. As if it had been converted into her very own jail cell. Panic trapped her in its iron grip, her mind thrashing, but her body remained as still as glass. She wanted to scream but couldn't. So, she just lied there in silence. Nothing but darkness around her. And then she faded away, yet again.

———

The next time Finley woke up, she didn't know what was happening. Her last moment of consciousness was fuzzy, remembering some kind of fear, but she couldn't seem to hold one thought in her mind long enough to figure out what it was.

She didn't know how long she'd been lying there, trying to string one sentence together in her head when her entire world was turned upside down. The floor beneath her back rattled and slid, and her body felt as if it were moving somehow. She tried to regain balance to open her eyes and see what was happening, but her body remained still around her.

A loud sound began to rattle in her ears, piercing her stiff eardrums and making her head ache. Her world exploded into muted light as she became aware of a lit room. Her eyes were still shut, but she could see through her lids the radiating luminescence that casted a red glow on her vision. She tried to move again, but it was in vain.

Instead, Finley tried to become more aware of the

things she could feel. She may be unable to move her body, but the nerves in her skin still received information that fed through to her mind. Her body felt bruised, her neck, arm, and pelvis all aching with a searing pain that suggested they had been broken. Some memories tickled at the back of her consciousness, but it faded as quickly as it had come. She wondered then, why she might've been injured. Had she been in an accident during one of her rounds in the district? Maybe she'd fallen from her bike.

Unable to recall anything, she returned to her skin. She was cold, though where her skin should have puckered, it remained still. It made the icy air feel like a heavy blanket weighing down over her body. The ground beneath her was also chilled, unaffected by her mass upon it. It was hard, but it didn't feel rough like stone.

Metal? She didn't know for sure.

The next thing she noticed was a lightweight blanket being lifted from her face. She knew it was a blanket because some of the weight on her body grew lighter, and she felt someone pull it back, the luminescence growing brighter, and someone above her. They were looking down at her silently, their breath barely audible. A sign that she wasn't alone. Wherever she was, other people inhabited it. Her first glimmer of hope.

Internally, she begged for the person to speak, to say something—anything to give her an idea of where she was or what was happening. She must've been there for hours, or at least, it seemed that way. And that presence never moved or changed. It just… hovered.

She felt the weight of their gaze, and occasionally,

felt their fingers ghosting just above her skin. But it was never firm enough for her to make it out as something more than wishful thinking. She was beginning to think that she'd just lie there forever when the presence shifted more audibly. She was still wondering what it was when she caught the sound of boots from another direction.

They sounded heavy. Stomped into the room, stopping just inches from her body. They remained silent for a moment, and then a man's voice sounded.

"You need to stop coming down here," he said, his tone quiet and commanding. He had the same air around him as the person standing over her, a stillness that wasn't inherently human. Or at least, not something natural to most people. Everyone she had ever known had a constant motion to them. Even when they weren't aware of it, they were moving, shifting, twitching. These people might as well not exist the second they stopped moving.

The person above her said nothing, but she sensed his hand move for the blanket. She wanted to scream at him to wait. To not put it back on her, to not forget about her. But her body was a useless weight to her. She didn't even twitch. The blanket went back on, and then the lights went out. And so did she.

———

This time, when Finley woke up again, she could remember the last few times she had been awake. She was in the dark, again, and it had given her time to think about what was happening. Her body was still paralyzed, but it hurt less than it had last time—which was a relief.

From the metal, she could feel the blanket placed on top of her. Probably a morgue. But it made no sense. If she were in a morgue, that would mean she was... dead.

But she didn't feel dead. She felt very much alive and conscious. Her memories were a bit fuzzy, but she was beginning to pick things up. She could remember Jenny going missing, finding Kingsley, and then the rebels. But after that, it was still all blank.

The last thing she could recall was retrieving the patients from the lab, being filled with tension and apprehension. Finley couldn't help but wonder where Kingsley would be if he knew where she was. And if she was ever going to be able to leave this place, where she seemed to float between life and death.

Was this what purgatory felt like? Sitting in a room and waiting for some divine being to come and collect her? Finley wasn't ready to die; she had so much fight still left in her. So many things she longed to complete. It infuriated her that she couldn't just open her eyes!

Her cheek twitched.

She froze.

She tried again. Nothing. Had she dreamt it? Made it up with her desperation? She tried again and again to move and still, nothing changed.

Then it happened again. It was tiny. Almost imperceptible. But it was there; it was hope.

———

She could move her finger. Just one, her left pointer finger. It was a barely-there lift of a limb, worth nothing in her day-to-day life. But right now? To Finley, it was bigger than anything had ever been.

Over the last few... whatever—she wasn't awake enough to know what time it was or how much of it had passed—she had been building up whatever strength she could. People had come and gone, and slowly, she picked up voices and started to recognize patterns of movement from the people around her.

They rarely ever took her out of her drawer, instead lingering outside, but the metal was thin enough for her to get the reverberation of their voices. Only on a few occasions was she ever removed, and she knew exactly who stood over her, quietly surveying every single time. It was Kingsley. She hadn't heard his speech since she'd woken up trapped within her flesh. He never made a peep. But she knew he was there from the quiet sound of his breathing and the almost there brush of his fingertips.

Finley always recognized Seneca in the same way, the stillness that was trained into them as mercenaries, so distinct in them. She recalled now how she had been captured by Ivan after the rescue mission, that she had been tortured and... killed. She remembered every cut and taunt in a weird two-way mirror.

Intellectually, he knew everything that had happened to her. She could feel the memories taking up space in her mind, like oil floating to the surface of water. But her emotional mind couldn't process them. She couldn't acknowledge the events or register them.

They just sat there, watching her like some beast in the shadows, threatening death while never moving an inch. It was its own kind of torture to Finley.

She was disturbed from her usual internal dialogue when she heard the familiar sound of Trench's boots coming down the wooden stairs to the morgue. Trench had been the third most common visitor in the morgue since she'd been here, following Kingsley and Seneca. She was as surprised by the woman's constant appearance as she had been by the mercenaries'.

Finley hadn't known any of the rebels well; she'd only been with them for a short amount of time. But she'd bonded with them over their shared goals and sense of injustice. The visits she occasionally got from Hunter or Bethany were what she expected, simply apologetic. But they had only lost a comrade, a friend perhaps, but not a sister nor a lover.

Seneca lingered around her resting place as if they had known each other for years. She heard him talking about the plans they were making, though most of it were imperceivable within the drawer. He apologized a lot, and it showed her a side of the man she had never seen. Every time he visited, she was more and more sorry that he had lost Ruby. And she wondered if he sympathize with Kingsley.

Trench also visited often, usually to rant about the state and its movements or how the patients were doing. Finley liked her visits the most because she never sounded sad, and for a few minutes, she could forget that she was a dead body inside a refrigerator and waiting to be disposed of. The idea always made her feel like she was about to have a panic attack, something more feasible if she were actually breathing.

Today, however, her finger moved. It was a step forward, and she was determined to somehow communicate with them. She didn't know if it was going to get better than this, but she did know that, slowly, her body seemed like it was healing, and every time she regained consciousness, she felt more present. She had to hold onto the hope that, someday, she would wake up.

Boots followed Trench into the room, enough that she found it hard to distinguish one from the other. She thought she recognized Ezra and Franko, but she couldn't be sure. There were others, a lot of others, and some she couldn't recognize.

Finley waited for the sound of the drawer opening, the sliding and shaking feeling of her tray being pulled out, and the sting of light behind her lids that she still couldn't see. There was the sound of muttering voices, broken through by Trench, who sounded upset.

The clicking and jarring of the drawer coincided with her loudly saying, "I know it sounds crazy, but you have to look!" And the coolness of air brushed against Finley's still legs as she was dragged out.

"This isn't funny!" Finley heard Hunter say, his voice weary.

"Good thing I'm not joking, then," Trench snapped back, her hand moving to the blanket that laid over Finley.

Finley strained forward mentally, screaming at the woman to remove the blanket. She could feel her finger tingling. She was ready; she just needed the damn cover off so people could see her when she moved.

"Trench, I know you're desperate. We all are, but this—it just isn't possible," Ezra stated, his tone sorrowful. Finley could feel Trench tense beside her, radiating with anger like gunpowder about to go off.

"Kingsley, tell them what we've seen. You know the bruises have been healing!" Trench cried over to Kingsley, but only silence replied to her.

A part of Finley broke, slightly hurt that Kingsley wouldn't fight for her. Finley had felt her body healing over time, her aches reducing and her mind clearing. She thought it was all in her head at first, but from what Trench said, maybe it was also happening for real. And if she had seen it, then Kingsley would've seen it as well—since he came to see her the most out of everyone. So, why wouldn't he say so?

Instead, it was Seneca who spoke up. "Trench has a point. I have noticed a reduction in bruising myself," he muttered quietly. The crowd grumbled, respecting the man as level-headed no matter the circumstance.

Franko spoke next. "It just isn't possible. She's dead! We saw her body, the injuries. No one could survive a fall off the wall into Antiqua-infested ground. Perhaps it's just the blood sinking in her body." But he sounded nervous, as if he were on edge about something.

Finley was worried that the fighting would carry on forever, but Trench went ahead and ripped the blanket away, revealing her body to the air. And Finley forced all her effort into moving that one little finger.

The people around her continued to argue, some of them convinced that she was indeed healing while others still denied everything. But Finley couldn't pay attention to any of that. Instead, she tensed her body, focusing all her energy toward one spot.

Her finger moved.

She waited for someone to notice. They didn't; they just kept arguing. She tried again and again, and all they did was continue to fight. Rage built up in Finley's chest. She had been to Hell and back, and she wasn't going to be defeated by the fact that they weren't paying enough attention.

In her head, she screamed at them. *Look at me! Look at me! Look at me!*

All the frustration she had ever possessed rose up within her and ran through her still veins. It was like an electric shock coursing through her, the world spinning with her fear. This couldn't fail. She couldn't go back into the drawer, presumed dead. She'd rot there forever! And eventually, everyone would stop visiting her, stop coming altogether. She'd be left forgotten.

These questions spun around in her mind again and again until she couldn't think straight, the noise around her both internal chaos and external anarchy.

And then her eyes opened, the light of the exposed bulb above burning into her retina. For a moment, it was stunning, so beautifully painful because she hadn't seen anything in what felt like such a long time. And then the ache set back in. She felt her heart beat against her chest, her lungs inflate, her muscles dormant. It hurt more than it had the first time she regained conscious-ness, but she embraced it. Because this was the pain of living, of existing.

From there, the chaos only continued. Finley could see people moving around her, their faces and voices bombarding her, but she couldn't pick them out properly. She had been stuck in the dark for so long that her body was overwhelmed by so much going on around her. Her entire being was filled with a tiredness that she couldn't describe, and it pulled at her mind to sleep. Finley resisted it, scared to fall asleep and perhaps never wake up again, but she fell in and out, the world around her swimming.

She was moved from the drawer, and she'd never been so happy to feel metal being pulled away from her skin. The next surface she was put on was soft and firm, a bed perhaps, and a much warmer blanket thrown over her, enough so the chills shaking her body began to settle.

Through all of it, there was one presence she could pick out—Kingsley's. Dark and silent next to her, but never moving away, and she clung to that as she finally let herself slip into slumber. Praying to any god out there that she would awaken again.

———

They were fighting about it *again*. Finley wanted to scream at them to shut the hell up, but her vocals were still recovering from what had been two months of stillness, managing only a groggy whisper in that moment. She watched as Hunter and Franko yelled at each other, each backed by their own half of the Core's main council. Kingsley sat quietly at Finley's side, a strong arm around her holding her up. He hadn't spoken to her since she came back to life, but he never left her either.

But she wanted to speak to him so badly, to beg for

him to forgive the promise she had made him keep, and for what he'd been through with her death, but he wouldn't look her in the eye. Wouldn't allow her to communicate with him in any way. And she hated it! Being so distant from him made her feel as if she'd never left the drawer. She squeezed his hand, trying to get some sort of reaction from him, but he didn't respond, not even turning to acknowledge her.

"She was infected with the vaccine!" Franko shouted. "We can't, in good conscience, let her roam around. She'll kill someone!"

"This is Finley we're talking about!" Bethany shouted back, her voice strained. "She's still recovering; we can't just chuck her into a cell to rot!"

"We can make it comfortable," Ezra pointed out subtly. He didn't like the idea of shutting the girl away, but he was worried for the rest of the people who stayed inside the building. And Finley couldn't say for sure that she didn't agree with him.

"We don't even know if she's going to turn," Trench protested, still sore from the way no one had believed her.

"She was… asleep, for two months," Franko continued. "Then she woke up, and it's been another month. Everyone turns after three months, and if anyone is infected, I think it's the one who… came back from the dead," he finished after much difficulty.

They all looked at Finley sheepishly, and she sighed.

In the time she had been awake, she told them all about the details of her torture, or the bits she could bring herself to talk about. Ivan had cut and beaten her until she was on the brink of death, then he'd wait for her to recover a bit before doing it all over again.

After three days of the same torture, he forcefully gave her the vaccine before throwing her across the wall. At that point, she had been close to death but aware enough to notice how the Antiqua hadn't attacked her. Instead, they wandered around her, looking at her as if she were some odd stone. At first, she'd been terrified, but after a while, she became curious.

If she tried to go near them, they backed away.

The Core had been as confused by the information as she had, and they still didn't know what to do with her. Finley skipped over the part where she had to drag her bleeding and broken body to one of the dumps near the wall and through the filth until she became unconscious. She hadn't talked about how she had lied there for hours, calling weakly for anyone to help her. How no one had come, how the night had set in, how the cold wind had burrowed so deep under her skin that her breaths finally stopped coming and her blood finally stopped pumping.

She remembered it all in such graphic detail that there were nights where she dreamt about it and woke up in sweat, worrying that this was some dream in the afterlife, and she was reliving her own death.

"Lock me up," Finley rasped, and the room went quiet.

Hunter turned his golden gaze on her, and she saw the guilt there. He didn't believe Trench, and he was thinking of what might've happened had the blanket never been removed. "You don't need to do that, Finley," he said. "We can find another way—"

"Don't be naïve," Finley interrupted him. He didn't need to stop talking. He could easily speak over her, but they all seemed hypersensitive to her presence. "I will turn tonight, and there is nothing that will change that. Lock me up."

Hunter looked down at the floor, refusing to meet her eyes, and so she turned to Seneca, who had been watching the fight with the same silent stillness as Kingsley. He just nodded and stepped forward, moving to lift Finley into his arms. She still couldn't walk on her own, and he tried to help take her to the place that others refused to take her. But before he could grab her, Kingsley lifted her into his arms, turning his back to block Seneca.

"Kingsley, please," Finley whispered softly, but he still refused to meet her gaze. He began to walk, and she was convinced that he'd take her somewhere other than where she wanted to go.

But she was surprised when he didn't, when he actually took her down to the cells—filled with aimless shapes of the others infected with the vaccine.

He placed her on top of a bed and stepped back, walking back toward the door. A part of her was still aching for him, sad that he wouldn't come back to her even though she had come back to him. And even though she asked for this, she wished he'd stay, even though she knew he couldn't.

But then he closed the door... from the inside, locking it and throwing the key onto the other side.

"Kingsley, what—" She began to ask, but he turned,

and she stopped when his green eyes met hers. Electricity ran through her at finally meeting eye-to-eye for the first time after so long. A tear slipped down her cheek, but she didn't stop it. She just watched as he sat down next to her, silently waiting with her as the sky darkened outside.

CHAPTER
TWENTY

After an hour, Finley was beginning to feel ill, and she wasn't happy with Kingsley's company anymore. At first, her heart warmed at the idea of him staying with her, but now she found anger bubbling inside her chest. He still hadn't spoken a word to her, and since he met her eyes after closing the door, he'd gone back to ignoring her. She shuffled away from him as much as her weak limbs would allow, which wasn't much considering they'd been atrophied for a solid eight weeks.

"Get out," she hissed with as much attitude as she could. He tried to reach for her, but she wouldn't let him. She *couldn't* let him. "Don't! Don't touch me, leave!" He hesitated and leaned back, still quiet. He didn't move any more than that, and she grimaced at the floor. "Go, Kingsley!" She was starting to scream now, her throat searing as she tried to force her voice to grow louder.

It wasn't until his hand touched her shoulder that she realized he'd moved closer to her again, and she flinched away. Slapping at the hand that tried to follow her, a fever began to spread over her body, and she felt the suffocation she was so familiar with now, sparking a wild desperation in her. To escape. To run. To flee.

"No!" she cried, then burst into tears. "I don't want to hurt you."

A spasm ran through her body, and her muscles contracted painfully, her vision wavering and a drunk feeling simmering at the edge of her consciousness. She was aware of Kingsley moving into her field of vision, but she found it hard to concentrate when another spasm shook her limbs.

"Finley?! Finley, look at me!" She heard Kingsley say, and somewhere inside, she rejoiced at the sound of his voice. Inside, she wanted to hug him, to love him again just because she could. Instead, she collapsed onto the floor, eyes to the ceiling as her body convulsed. She could tell that Kingsley was scared, but she didn't know what else she could do. She had been fighting the inevitable for so long. Perhaps it was time to give up.

———

Kingsley knew when she was gone, her eyes blank, and the blackness taking over their hazel depths. Her facial muscles finally relaxed after being strung so tight that he was worried she might snap one of her own bones. And for a second, she looked lifeless, so similar to the state she was in when he originally found her outside the wall. Memories of that day still plagued him, and he felt himself being pulled into the depths of those nightmares. But he fought to stay present, for her sake.

He knew his silence had been eating away at Finley over the past month, but he'd gone into some sort of coma when she died, retreated so far within himself that when she woke up again, he couldn't believe that he wasn't living in some kind of dream. That he was still asleep somewhere or dead, and this was in fact Heaven.

He couldn't bear the thought that it could even be a possibility. That for a moment, Finley was gone from this world. Unreachable, her soul dust against the wind. And he knew she had ghosts left from it. He saw it in the bruises under her eyes and the incessant way she tapped her foot when she was alone for more than a second. She was plagued by memories he couldn't help her with.

He couldn't remove them, wind back time and stop it all from happening. Just as with their childhood, her life had been scarred, and he, once again, failed to save her from any of it.

And so, he stayed silent, basking in her company whenever he could. He figured that if he didn't speak, he couldn't harm her any more than he had. He would just be there for her, the arm she could rest on and the protector she needed. She had her own demons lurking in her mind, and he didn't want to add on to that.

"Finley," he whispered softly, his voice cracking, but it was too late. The pain she showed on her face wasn't purely from the vaccine running through her veins. It had, yet again, been caused by him, and he wondered if he could ever be anything but a burden to her. "Please, Finley, open your eyes," he begged. He had to make things right. He couldn't bury himself in the grave of his own guilt; it was too much for any man to carry.

He jolted backwards when she sat up abruptly, climbing to her feet with more strength than she should've had. She had been struggling to walk on her own, let alone lift herself from the ground and stand strong on her own legs. He stared up at her, a part of him hoping he'd see Finley looking back at him.

She'd awoken from the dead; at this point, anything was possible. But that part of him faded when he saw that blank look in her eyes.

He stood slowly, and she watched him with the keen gaze of a falcon that watches its prey scurry across the grass from miles above. Every twitch, every breath, she watched it all and waited. Around him, he heard the other vaccinated begin to holler in unrest, banging against the bars to get to each other, screaming and growling like feral animals. Even after all these years of watching patient after patient turn, he still couldn't get used to the deafening sounds they made. They didn't sound angry, never angry. Only as if they were in pain from their organs liquifying inside them, and they were trying to climb out of their own skin. It was haunting.

When Finley remained still, he put his arms out in

front of him as he would if approaching a wild animal, taking slow steps toward her, watching for any sign of attack. She remained still, swaying lightly on her feet.

When he was close enough, Kingsley tentatively laid a hand on her shoulder, wanting to sigh in relief when he felt her skin warm beneath his hand. During the months that Finley was dead, he had visited her, again and again, just to stare at her. He'd always wanted to touch her, to feel her skin beneath his own, but he could never bring himself to fully do so.

He had touched a dead body before, too many. And he knew the cold paleness of their skin. He didn't think he could keep himself together if he felt *her* skin cold. He'd been hanging to clarity by a thread, and he knew that if he allowed himself to accept that she was gone, he would have dropped into a threatening dark abyss.

Now he chanted in his mind again and again that she was alive, breathing and moving beneath his touch. She turned to look at him, her face smooth of the lines of fatigue and upset that had been present moments before.

"Fin—"

She slammed her body against him, ramming him into the wall behind him. He felt the air *whoosh* from his chest, leaving him choking, and his back stung from where it had hit the stone. He barely had enough time to register what had happened before she began to swing at him, scratching with her nails and gnashing with her teeth. It was only by the grace of his mercenary training that he defended himself on instinct, his mind still reeling.

She was stronger, much more than she had ever

been before her untimely death, more so than the patients he had fought before. He struggled to push her away, her claws catching his skin and drawing fine lines of blood that pooled and dripped. Her teeth went for his neck, and he was forced to push back, flipping her so that she lied on her back against the floor. She didn't groan in pain as she normally would; she didn't make any snarky comment or smile at him in that cheeky way she usually did.

Instead, she screamed, one of those terrifying screeches that dug its way so far into his brain that he swore he could feel her scratching at his spine.

It was like nails on a chalkboard.

Taking advantage of her vulnerable position, Kingsley sat on her chest, using his body weight and legs to restrain her arms and immobilize her. She thrashed beneath him, nearly unseating him, but he held fast, ignoring the way her fingers dug into his thighs deep enough to pierce the skin.

He put a hand onto her face, following it as she moved and twitched endlessly, frothing at the mouth like a rabid dog.

"Finley," he gasped, "please, please, come back to me!" His voice was pitchy with tears. He had finally found her after so long, after making so many mistakes, and just like that, he managed to ruin it again. He had her in his grasp, and he failed to keep her safe time after time. Now, once again, he was facing the idea of a future without her, and he couldn't stand it.

"You have to wake up, Finley!" Tears were falling freely from his eyes now and pattering onto her face, each drop rolling down her cheeks as if they were her own. He let himself sob as he spoke to her thrashing form. "I never forgot you, Finley. Never! I thought of you every day, of joining you wherever you were. I thought you were dead, and it was all my fault for not keeping you safe, for not stopping my father… or at least trying."

He stroked her beneath one of her eyes and noticed that she herself was beginning to cry, though they were unfocused and crazed. "I need you to know that I love you. I want to go back in time and be there for you, to change everything, to give you the family that you deserve." His words choked off at the end, and he buried his head into her neck, crying until he was breathless. Finley continued to wail beneath him, the wetness of her tears soaking into his shirt.

"I'm sorry, Finley. I'm so sorry."

He didn't know how long he had lied there, only that the world around him seemed to fade away, and a numbness began to settle in. He whispered again.

"I'm sorry."

But nothing changed.

He was then shaken out of his stupor by a hand on his back. Fury raged through him at the thought of someone coming into her cell. It was for her safety as much as theirs that she was locked in here.

But when he looked behind him, there was no one, just the empty hall and the sight of other patients mindlessly trying to escape from their own cells. It wasn't until he heard a sniffle that he looked down.

Finley was looking up at him, face once again tired, tears rolling down her cheeks. She was writhing; she wasn't groaning or screaming. She was looking at him with such utter sadness that it hollowed out his heart.

Then she spoke. "Kingsley?" And a smile drew wide across his face, scooping her up into his arms and clutching her to his chest.

"Thank, God," he gasped, "I thought I had lost you."

She groaned, and he looked down, releasing his arms slightly when he realized he was clutching her too tightly for her fragile state. She rubbed at her forehead. "I feel like I've been hit with a train," she whispered, her voice even more torn from her screaming. He chuckled.

"So do I," he agreed, and she smiled at him. But the moment of peace was short-lived, and a frown quickly overtook her.

"Did I—Did I change?" she asked, and he paused before nodding, his face downcast. She seemed to take the news well, but he could see parts of her fracturing underneath. "Did I hurt you?"

He shook his head vehemently. "No more than I hurt you," he said, and tears began falling down her cheeks again. He pulled her back to his chest, more gently this time, and rubbed her back. "Why are you crying?"

"It's just—It's so nice to hear your voice," she mumbled.

"I'm sorry," he said again, though he didn't know if she had heard him the first two times. "I'm so—"

She placed a finger to his lips. "I heard you," she whispered. "Through everything. The fog that came over me, I heard you. You brought me back."

He shot her a look, a look he wasn't sure represented shock or wonder.

"Don't look so surprised! I actually like you, you know?" she continued.

It was his turn to smile, and he idly noticed how easy it was summoned around her. "I like you, too," he whispered into her hair, the moment feeling too delicate to speak any louder.

"I thought you liked me a bit more than that," she teased, bringing her finger to his chin, forcing him to look her in the eyes. "You said you love me."

"I do," he said without hesitation, and the smile it summoned was enough to blind him.

"I love you, too," she whispered breathily, but something twinged in his mind, and he frowned, looking away.

"You shouldn't," he said. "After what I've done to you, your family, I don't deserve your love."

"Don't do that," she retorted, her tone strong enough to make him glance back at her. She looked angry, which confused him. "Don't you dare retreat from me. You've been running away since you realized who I was. You say you don't want to hurt me again. Well, now's your chance. Stick around and face the consequences, and let me love you as much as I damn well want to!" She was losing her breath from her rant, but she kept going. "And just so you know, I don't forgive you, for any of it. Which is why you're gonna stick around until I decide when you've made it up to me!" She stuck her bottom lip out like a stubborn child, and he grinned slightly despite the somber mood.

"And how long will that take?" he asked.

She gave him an overexaggerated pondering look. "I don't know… maybe forever?"

Kingsley laughed, leaning his forehead against hers.

"What are we going to do now?" he asked after a while of comfortable silence, soaking in her presence. But they couldn't run from reality forever, and the truth of their situation was still rattling around them.

She sighed, but then looked up at him before lifting herself to her feet. He watched, slack-jawed, but she tugged at him to join her. She was unsteady, but she managed to stand on her own two feet. She looked at him with such assurance, that for a moment, he believed they were going to be fine.

"We rally everyone together, everyone who can fight, hold a gun or a weapon, and we form an army. The sanctum is on lockdown; they're looking inwards, so now is our time to escape." Finley finally spoke, holding her chin high with assurance.

"How? The Antiqua outside the wall will kill us for sure," Kingsley asked.

But she shook her head, a darkness shifting over her eyes before vanishing. "No, the Antiqua don't recognize those with the vaccine as humans. We have enough patients here to form a protective shield around those uninfected. Then we'll find somewhere safe, where we can start fresh!"

Her eyes looked dreamy as if she were imagining some far-off place, but he couldn't stop himself from asking questions about her strategy. He was a calculated mind, after all, plus he wasn't very good at taking orders. "But how will we take the patients without them killing us or each other? They're catatonic during the day and rabid, at best, at night."

"We'll wake them up."

"How—" She put another finger to his lips.

"You woke me up. Now it's time to wake the others, and get the hell out of here."

And as much as Kingsley wanted to believe in her, in them, there was still that little voice in the back of his mind, warning him that this could all go very, very wrong.

CHAPTER
TWENTY-ONE

Everyone thought she was crazy, and in a way, Finley understood why. She knew that if she'd heard herself speak a few months ago, she would've told herself to jump off the wall headfirst. What she was proposing was idiotic, insane, suicidal!

But she also couldn't help but think that it was the right thing to do. And after the many near misses she'd been through, nearly dying time after time, she was beginning to think she had a lucky cricket on her shoulder.

She had faith in herself, and Kingsley had faith in her. They had become much closer since she'd nearly turned just over two weeks ago. The confession he made to her when she was crazed still echoed in her mind, and she tried her hardest to convince him that he didn't need to feel such a burden for everything. He had been a child as well, and they were only human.

But no matter how many times she tried to comfort him, he wouldn't let her take his burden from him. He loved her, with an intensity that scared her sometimes, but he also tortured himself, and it broke her just to watch.

They had been inseparable, though. They slept in the same bed, ate at the same time, and he never asked her where she was going or why. He just helped her get to where she needed to be.

Finley had pushed herself to her physical limits. Her limbs were still weak, but the night she changed proved that she had the strength inside of her somewhere. It had been grueling and painful, but she was back on her feet now. Not as strong as she had been before, but she could hold herself in a fight again, and she was determined not to be a disadvantage to the Core.

She spent her time while rehabilitating herself teaching the other infected patients how to regain some of their consciousness. But it'd been nothing but hopeless. None of them responded to her, and she was beginning to think she would never reach them.

But then she remembered what bought her back, Kingsley, his voice, his presence. For each patient, she found a loved one of theirs and got them to return again and again, talking to them and encouraging them to return to their body.

It took a while, but after a few days, the patients started coming back, and Finley could finally begin training them to control the vaccine. In the end, it gave them an advantage. The vaccine made them stronger and more durable, and if they could use that against the state, then they had a chance of winning.

———

And finally, that day arrived, the day they were going to start their fight for freedom. Everyone was twitchy, feeling jumpy and scared. And she couldn't blame them. What they were about to try was so dangerous that it almost looked like a disaster, but they had come so far already that Finley didn't think there was anything else they could do. Their people were dying, some of the hybrids had been so far gone that they couldn't be saved, and they had to be put down. And it just wasn't right that they had to suffer just so a bunch of rich pricks could have slaves to do their dirty work.

No, she gritted her teeth. *This will end today. And however the penny drops, the state will not come out of it on top.*

Finley walked into the council room where everyone waited. Kingsley smiled at her and joined her by her side as she stepped up to the table, where everyone looked toward her for her input. On the table in front of them was a map of the city, small figures dictating where their forces laid and where the state's were.

Hunter stood in her presence and nodded his head;

she nodded back before sitting.

"We have a problem," Hunter said, his golden eyes grim, and she quirked a brow in question. "With the number of soldiers we have compared to the firepower the state holds, we'll never get everyone over the wall safely. Our hybrids will have to help fight as the strongest amongst us, but they also must protect those outside the wall from Antiqua… we're at a stalemate!" He cringed and rubbed the bridge of his nose.

Finley stared at the map, her eyes wandering from one end to the other. Hunter was right. They were a force to be reckoned with, but the state had the mercenaries and their guns, and the Core's resources would be stretched too thin. She focused in on the wall, a thick line representing the thing that trapped them all on this side, like rats stuck in a well and scrabbling over each other to escape.

If only the damn thing wasn't there… she pondered.

An idea sparked.

"We get rid of the wall," she finally stated, and silence greeted her. The eyes around the table stared blankly.

"Well—" Ezra began, but she cut him off.

"Trench, do you still have that gunpowder?" Finley asked, and the woman nodded, her face stoic. "Do you think it can blow through the wall?"

Trench stared at the map, her gaze intense before a small grin appeared on her lips. "Yeah," she drawled, "if it's concentrated enough. I could blow a hole big enough to get out."

Finley nodded, turning back to the others. "We'll blow a hole, which eliminates the issue of climbing, then we head right on out." She gestured casually to the map.

Franko spoke up next. "Not to rain on your parade, but what do we do when the Antiqua come pouring inside?" He sounded sarcastic, and she shot him a look. Franko had been the most resistant to her plan since the very beginning, and he always seemed to undermine her at every turn.

"Our hybrids will protect our people. The Antiqua can be lured toward the sanctum and act as cannon fodder. They'll also offer us some coverage in getting people out."

Franko looked annoyed that she had answered him so quickly, but Finley basked in the approving looks that Seneca and the others were giving her.

"It means we're going to have to split our forces again." Seneca pointed out but was interrupted by Kingsley.

"No," he said, looking at Finley with stone in his eyes. She gave him a sympathetic look, putting her hand softly on his, but he pulled away. "We aren't separating again, not after last time."

"Kingsley—You need to help our soldiers. Aside from Seneca, you know their forces better than anyone, and I'm…" Finley paused, her pride stinging. "I'm not strong enough to be on the front lines. I'll be a liability. I'll help the civilians escape."

He frowned, moving to cling onto her arm. "I can't lose you again," he said so softly that the others at the table couldn't hear him.

"This is the last time I will ask this of you," Finley promised, but she knew he was still hurting. She could tell he didn't want to let her go. After the trauma of nearly losing her so many times, she could understand his worry.

But this was bigger than them. And they had to think of the people.

He nodded finally, after staring at her intently for a moment. She thanked him with her eyes before turning back to the table.

"We separate into two groups. The soldiers attack the sanctum, hold them off while we blow through the wall and evacuate. The Antiqua will flood in, and the hybrids working with the others will aid them in also evacuating. The two groups will then re-join outside the wall and begin our trek south, toward the Endian mountains," Finley explained to the group, motioning precisely at the map.

Everyone nodded, but there was an air of dread in the room. They all knew the risk they were about to take, and every single one of them was prepared to die for their cause.

But the question remained, would it be enough?

———

It took a few hours and some difficult goodbyes, but eventually, everyone was in place when light turned to dark. The tension ran throughout the city, which sat still and silent, every street empty, every home dark. The people were either part of the revolution or inside the sanctum. There were only two sides to this fight, and violence ran like a song through the air. Finley wasn't sure she couldn't smell the blood already.

She paused outside the Core's building, her small pack on her back, everything she would bring with her to her new life. She'd gathered those from her district, but she hadn't been able to find Mag. People told her she was amongst the civilians somewhere, that she would turn up, but Finley couldn't help but worry for her adoptive mother. She had lost one mother before; she wasn't sure she could handle losing another.

Kingsley stepped up beside her, his body draped in black and looking as he had when she first met him. She had gotten so used to him in normal clothes—the ones that had been given to him by the Core—that the leather looked odd on him now. His face was blank, but she could tell that he was just as nervous as she was.

Silently, she reached her hand toward his, linking one of her fingers with his own. People flooded out from behind them, heading in one of two directions. Toward the wall or toward the sanctum.

The time was now, but Finley couldn't help but wish she could have one more night with Kingsley, to lie in his arms and feel the pleasure he wrought from her body. He was hypnotic and consuming, and she wasn't convinced she could ever have enough of him. But she pushed aside the desire for what she knew was coming ahead.

She turned her head toward him and found him already looking at her. She wanted to say goodbye, to make sure that he knew she loved him. But she couldn't bring herself to do so. It seemed finite, and his eyes looked like she was already breaking his heart.

Instead, she leapt into his arms and kissed him, their lips pressed together and their tongues danced, sharing a breath one last time. She felt so wrapped up in him that she couldn't tell where he began and where she ended.

And then Finley found herself turning and walking away. She didn't look back, and she didn't say goodbye. Because if she was going to get through the fight ahead of her, she had to believe that she would see him again, and they would be free to never fight again once her people were safe.

———

By the time Finley reached the wall, the sounds of fighting had erupted behind her, and she tried not to let herself think about Kingsley being there in the center of it all. Gunshots rang out in the dark, their firing light creating an ominous luminescence in the distance, and she could tell the civilians were getting scarred, the wails of children and adults alike echoing in the night.

But Finley couldn't let herself focus on any of that; she had to stay strong. For everyone. Trench greeted her first. She looked serious, unlike the sassy woman she knew her to be, and her brows were creased in worry.

"Is it ready?" Finley asked, not addressing the woman's concern.

Trench nodded, and they walked to the blast site, the ammunition linked and ready for ignition. Bethany was also with them, alongside her brother, and they were all dressed in black. Their clothes, combined with their face, made it feel like a funeral, and Finley couldn't help the stab of guilt that pierced through her. This was her idea, her plan. If they died… it would be her head.

She shook the thought away and signaled with her hand toward the hybrid soldiers that made a barricade around the civilians, everyone preparing for the blast. There was a click in the silence, the singular light drawing everyone's gaze. The line ignited, sizzling and spitting, and everyone watched as it traveled down. Closer and closer to the gunpowder.

They expected it to blow at any minute, but it just sizzled and traveled at a leisurely pace, as if ignoring the tension around it. Finley counted down in her head —five, four, three, two, one…

Everything went dark again. People held their breath, waiting for a blast that didn't come. Someone turned their head to ask a question, but they were silenced when the wall lit up with flames. The resounding boom was enough to burst Finley's eardrums, and she could see from the winces on every-one's face that they had felt the same pain.

Smoke and dust billowed like a vengeful spirit, coloring the sky with red haze, but as the wall cleared, Finley spotted the sand dunes behind it, the rolling hills that led into the distance.

Everyone froze, completely raptured by the site of space, going on forever with no barriers or buildings. Hope rose up within everyone like a tangible feeling, and the crowd bristled with curiosity. That was until the first scratch pierced the night, then another… and another.

And it wasn't long until the Antiqua began pouring through the gap. They were rotting and horrifying, their bodies long past their prime, arms and legs missing, eyes hanging from sockets, and skulls peeled back. The gore and smell were enough to turn Finley's stomach, and she heard more than one person puke.

Everyone huddled in fear as the Antiqua wandered past, some quicker than others. A few showed interest in the crowd, inquisitively shuffling closer, but the second they got near a hybrid, they wailed and changed their course.

In just under an hour, the Antiqua had mostly passed through, and only stragglers remained, enough that the crowd could begin moving through the gap. People rushed forward, both scared and hopeful, the tension visible in their tear-tracked face and eyes wide with terror. They were running into a future they couldn't predict. It was the ultimate gamble.

Trench, along with Bethany, went to the front of the group, leading them all out and finding a safe place to wait for the soldiers, but Ezra hesitated alongside Finley.

"Are you not coming?" he asked, his eyes assessing. But Finley couldn't bring herself to smile for him, not even in this moment of apparent success.

"I—" she hesitated, not knowing how to articulate what she was feeling. But the older man nodded before she could say anything.

"You can't leave him." He sighed. "Neither can I," and it was then that Finley felt connected to the man next to her. Hunter and Ezra had been like brothers to her, but they were comrades with a common goal.

They hadn't bonded as she had with Trench and Seneca. But now, she saw them simply as two men in love, praying that they would make it another day to see each other again.

They were still staring at each other when a blast sounded in the distance, much louder than anything that should've been coming from that area. When they looked over, they saw flames reaching high into the night sky and heard the sound of screams, both human and monster, crawling through the darkness.

Finley's breath froze in her lungs, and she was running before she even knew what was happening, her legs pumping, aching much sooner than they should have, and she felt anger burn down her throat at her slowness. Ezra jogged beside her, but she could tell he wanted to run ahead. Others would have, but he was a compassionate man, and he wouldn't leave her behind to defend herself.

Then, out of the corner of her eye, she noticed a motorcycle parked on the side of the street, the silver beats left abandoned, and she felt a smile take over her face. She jogged toward it, feeling Ezra's confused look but not finding the breath to explain it to him. She simply threw her leg over the saddle and began to fiddle with the wires she popped out from its neck. Within seconds, it was roaring to life. She glanced at Ezra, who watched her with wide eyes.

"Hop on!" she shouted, and he didn't hesitate, his large body taking up the back of the bike.

They spun around on the pavement, the back wheel squealing on the concrete before taking off down the street fast enough to make Finley's eyes water. But she didn't close them or slow down. No, she stepped on the gas as hard as she could, zooming toward the chaos in the center of the city.

As they approached, more and more Antiqua

became visible, until there were so many that she struggled to dodge them. Many of them tried to reach for Ezra as they passed through, but Finley managed to maneuver around them with speed.

A few blocks from the mayhem, they had to abandon the bike; the Antiqua were everywhere. Finley pulled Ezra to higher ground, and they managed to make it a few blocks until they found themselves in the middle of the fight.

A gas tank must've ignited somewhere because the area was littered with fire, smoke billowing into the night. Gunshots rang out from everywhere, and those not using guns slashed at others with knives. Antiqua was amongst it all, tearing friend and foe alike to shreds, and Finley had to stop herself from jumping in to save everyone, no matter how much it called to her.

She searched the crowds for Kingsley, but it was hard to tell one person apart from the other. The black figures of mercenaries shifted everywhere she looked, their deadly skills cutting down everything in their path. It was blood-curdling to watch, but she put faith in the idea that Kingsley would be prepared to fight for himself. For them.

Finley and Ezra were halfway down the street when she heard the thwack of flesh on flesh behind her. She turned just in time to see an Antiqua tackle Ezra to the ground, grappling for him. He was big, and he fought the beast off, but another came, and then another. Finley scrambled for him, trying desperately to reach him.

"Ezra!" she screamed, pain lacing her throat. His eyes flickered to her, and she nearly sobbed when she saw the acceptance in his eyes.

"Go!" he shouted, but she couldn't leave him. She tried again to reach him, but there were bodies everywhere, and she still wasn't as strong as she used to be. She caught his eyes once more through the writhing bodies and saw the pain in his eyes, the blood dripping from the corner of his mouth as the Antiqua began to feast on his flesh.

"Go!" Ezra roared, and she never heard him sound so angry, so heartbroken.

There were so many Antiqua now, their flesh pressed against hers, their bloody skin sticking to her clothes. They forced her back, so forcefully that even when he began to scream, and she tried again and again to break through, she was too weak. And she was pushed further back until his screams had faded, and her limbs were too weak to push anymore.

Tears ran down her face, and she sent up a silent prayer for the man whose heart was bigger and warmer than anyone she'd ever met. But with the chaos raining down around her, she couldn't linger for long. The Antiqua were swarming, and if she wasn't careful, they'd trample right over her.

Spinning around, Finley tried to see if she could spot Kingsley again, but there were so many creatures around her that she could see nothing but the fire and buildings looming over them like silent gods, watching as their own tore each other apart.

Determined, she ran for a car that had been left abandoned on the street, climbing on top to lift herself above the crowd. The red metal sunk in beneath her feet, but she ignored it, lifting herself up on trembling legs. The Antiqua formed a sea of writhing bodies around her, so thick that she couldn't see the ground beneath their feet.

They clawed at each other and feasted on what she assumed were bodies lying beneath them, but she avoided looking too closely. The figures of those alive and moving were growing precariously few, and Finley dreaded to accept that most of their soldiers were gone. Dead or fleeing, she had no idea.

She spun again and again, looking for anything to hold onto, but everything around her swam with blood and flesh. Her head rattled from within, her mind bogged down by panic and grief.

And then she spotted him. Even from a yard away, she knew it was him, could see it in his posture and sleek fighting style. He didn't see her, but he was fighting swiftly, cutting down the monsters in front of him.

But that relief was short-lived when she spotted Strage and his goon, Ivan, heading toward him. They took down the Antiqua that stood in their way, and Kingsley had no idea they were coming for him. His back was turned, and the noise of the screams and fire around them was loud enough to block out any noise Finley managed to make.

"Kingsley!" she screamed, jumping and waving her arms, praying that he'd see her. He didn't. "Kingsley, behind you!" she tried again, but her voice was quickly dying, and Kingsley still heard nothing.

Finley plunged into the crowd, forcing her way through the bodies and ignoring the crunch of things beneath her feet or the hands that groped for her. She reached Ivan first, his back turned to her as he cut down

Antiqua after Antiqua that tried to rip his skin from his body. He already had several bad cuts on his face and arms, and Finley couldn't help the feeling of sick satisfaction that rose within her.

At the sight of Ivan, memories flooded back to her, the pain she had felt in his company, her begging screams as he laughed while he broke her bones and her pride. He had desecrated her body in the worst way, giving her that vile vaccine and hurling her off the wall, leaving her to die.

It was because of him that she was weak, that she couldn't save Ezra or fight alongside Kingsley.

Using the rage that gave her energy, she pummeled into his back, throwing him off his balance and into the Antiqua he had been fighting off. Immediately, they began to pull at his skin, taking chunks from it like piranhas in a swamp. Ivan screamed and thrashed, reaching for the blade he had dropped. But just as he put his hand on it, Finley placed her boot on his fingers. Digging down until they crunched, and he squealed.

His eyes shot over to her, and pure hatred looked back at her.

"I killed you," he spat, and she smiled demonically.

"What was it that you promised?" She taunted, taking pleasure in the slow way the Antiqua began consuming his flesh. "You're going to peel the skin from my body? Well, let me return the favor." And then she pushed her boot into his chest, his head falling beneath the wave of Antiqua as they piled on top of him. His screams vanished within a second, and only the wet sound of flesh and bones breaking remained.

She was distracted from her revenge, though, when

she spotted Strage moving far too quickly through the bodies toward Kingsley, who was struggling with another onslaught of ravenous mouths. Fear spiked in her blood, and she ran toward them, again calling out for him but remaining unheard.

Finley reached Strage first, whose giant body loomed above her, unnatural muscles tensing and releasing with precise swings. She used the element of surprise to swipe his legs out from under him, but her muscles screamed, depleted from all the fighting she'd already done.

Strage swung for her, and she avoided his blade by a mere hairbreadth, the blade cutting through the front of her top above her stomach. If he'd hit her, she'd be holding her guts in about now. That is, if the Antiqua didn't begin feasting on her organs the second they smelled blood.

She tried to throw blows back at him, but he was much faster and stronger, his skills above her own, and no matter how hard she tried, he always seemed to move back closer and closer to Kingsley.

Finley growled, and for the first time, Strage looked her in the eyes, acknowledging her presence more than that of a fly in his way. And she felt herself shake under the weight of his stare. It felt as if it were digging through her skull, rifling in her thoughts. At that moment, she wished she hadn't laid eyes upon him, and she knew it would haunt her forever.

"You little worm," he drawled, his voice so low that she felt it vibrate through her. "I'm going to crush you under my boots."

But his words only sparked her temper to life, and

she grinned like a feral cat. "Not if I do it first," and then she lunged forward, renewed by her anger and determination to kill this man—who was more of a monster than all the flesh-eating Antiqua that surrounded them.

They traded blow after blow, each missing and hitting in equal measure. Within minutes, she was panting, blood trickling down her leg from one of his cuts. Her only saving grace was that Strage himself was breathing heavier, and he sported his own cuts on his cheek and hand. They watched each other and circled, waiting for the other to strike. It was then that something caught her eye. Glinting from behind Strage, the dull metal a beacon in the craziness of this fight.

And it was in that moment that Finley knew what she needed to do. Kingsley needed to live, and he wouldn't if she didn't kill Strage. But she was so tired, so weak. She knew that no matter how hard she fought, he would beat her in the end. Resolved, she began to pace forward, picking up speed as she went until she was sprinting.

Purposely, she threw her form off, and she saw the glint in Strage's eyes, which told her he had noticed and thought he was about to get the upper hand.

Think again, asshole.

She hit him with full force, their bodies clashing, and he rolled her just as she knew he would, her smaller and more fragile body collapsing beneath the mass of his. She felt the sting of his blade as it pierced her gut, and she tried to ignore the way her flesh ripped in its wake. Her body exploded in pain, but it was nothing she hadn't felt before. She then looked into

Strage's black eyes and the satisfaction he held there. He thought he had won.

Good.

She coughed as blood pooled in her throat, the red liquid bubbling from her lips and dripping from her mouth.

"You should have accepted your fate, you stupid child," he groaned, his victory speech all prepared. "You could've served an empire, and instead, you'll rot underground like an insect."

As he spoke, Finley reached one hand above her, moving slowly from where she had landed on it. It sparked with agony, enough to tell her it was probably broken, but she didn't let anything show on her face. She just moved inch by inch while Strage babbled on about the glory of the state and how much of a pig she was.

But she didn't care. His words meant nothing, and as the blood drained out of her body, a euphoric numbness seeped into her limbs.

She only knew her hand had landed on the gun when she felt its cold weight. She gripped it like a lifeline and allowed another sweet smile to cover her face, and internally, she rejoiced at the discomfort it sparked in the man above her.

"I'll see you in Hell," she muttered before drawing the gun up between them and pulling the trigger. Strage's face was blown away, parts of his skull and brain spewing out from his head, and it was enough to force him to throw his body from hers, stopping his dead weight from trapping her on the ground.

Immediately, Antiqua swarmed above him, digging

into his corpse, and Finley was only sad that he hadn't suffered longer. He deserved to die torturously, but there were bigger things at stake now.

She was fighting, not for her future alone, but for her people. So that they could live in harmony, free from the chains of the state. They would live off the land, sharing labor and living together in happiness. Her children would play on the grass without the fear of someone coming along to take them away. They would grow up knowing that the land around them was as much theirs as anyone else's. And they would sing and play in a care-free manner that Finley never had herself. The future she saw for everyone was one where violence didn't exist, where no human was above another.

That was what she fought for.

Looking around, she tried to find Kingsley again, but there were too many creatures around her, and the fire and smoke clouded her vision. She held her hand to her stomach, knowing she couldn't remove the knife unless she wanted to bleed to death.

But she also knew she couldn't move with it in. Gritting her teeth, she yanked at it, the blade slipping free like butter. Blood rushed from the wound, pouring from her injury, and her head swam, darkness kissing at the edge of her vision. She took off her jacket and pressed it to the wound. It didn't help much, but it might keep her alive long enough to find help. She took a step forward, but stopped when she saw an Antiqua running for her. She was confused at first because none of the Antiqua targeted those with the vaccine.

Then she realized it was one of the hybrids, their

dark clothes marking them as one of her own. The woman's face was mad, blood smeared around her mouth and pooled from her eyes and ears. She screamed as she ran, and Finley could think of nothing else but to lift her gun and shoot. The woman went down in three shots, the final one on her head.

Finley stared at the woman's body, her heart thudding in her chest. The chaos of the fight had started to convert some of the hybrids back to their original form, and she hoped, yet again, that the civilians were at least safe. She continued to push her way through the crowd, but she became increasingly weaker, the shots she took at the hybrids sloppy at best.

Fifteen minutes later, she took down her eighth hybrid before the gun ran out of ammo, clicking uselessly in her grip. She looked around frantically for any sign of Kingsley, but he was gone, and she was all alone, surrounded by corpses and flames. Finally, she let the weakness of her legs take her, and she fell onto her knees, feeling the slow bubble of blood leaving her system.

She must've blacked out because the next time she opened her eyes, she was on the ground, her cheek resting on cold concrete, feet and legs surrounding her like the trees of a forest. Or at least, what she could recall of a forest since she hadn't seen once since she was just a young girl. She was fading in and out, her mind far away with her mother and her father in her childhood home, playing with the toy dragons and knights they had gotten her for her birthday, when she saw something shift a few feet away.

She cleared her vision enough, rubbing at her eyes

with sodden hands until she saw him, also lying on the ground, his body still and bloody a few feet away.

Finley sobbed when she saw Kingsley's empty eyes, his gaze cloudy, blood dried around his mouth. She couldn't see the blow that had ended him, but it was clear to her that he was gone. Sobbing, she began to drag herself across the ground, using what little strength she had remaining until she was close enough to take the hand that stretched out in front of him. She no longer had the will to move, her blood more on the ground around her than inside of her, and she could feel her heart flutter, trying to pump nothing but air through her veins.

She gripped Kingsley's hand in her own, crying out when she felt his cold skin beneath her own. She couldn't process it all, that he was gone, that the boy she had loved was really dead. They had so little time together. There were so many things she wished they could've done, words they could've shared, and a future they could've built.

It wasn't fair. None of this was fair. They deserved a happy ending; they deserved a happily ever after where they ran off into the sunset. They had played their part in this whole apocalypse and clung to each other like boats to lighthouses during a storm. This was not how their story should've ended.

But it seemed like that wasn't up to Finley anymore, and the last thing she saw, as blackness grabbed at her consciousness, were Kingsley's eyes staring into her own, the love he had for her conveyed even in death.

ABOUT THE AUTHOR

Viola Tempest is a dystopian fantasy and paranormal romance author who yearns to expose the truth of those in the modern world: the good, the bad, and the ugly. Her inspiration primarily stems from life experiences, those who annoy her, ex-boyfriends, and the crazy dreams that pop into her head every once in a while.

STALK HER BELOW!

Website:
https://www.violatempest.com/

Facebook Page:
https://www.facebook.com/authorviolatempest

Instagram:
https://www.instagram.com/author_violatempest/

Goodreads:
https://www.goodreads.com/author/show/
21693342.Viola_Tempest

Bookbub:
https://www.bookbub.com/authors/viola-tempest

THE WRATH OF NIGHT

VIOLA TEMPEST